MY BIG FURRY ALIEN SATYR

STARLIGHT MONSTERS
BOOK 2

SKYE MACKINNON

Peryton Press

MY BIG FURRY ALIEN SATYR

SKYE MACKINNON

CONTENTS

To Tricia, my lovely assistant,

and to Valkyrie, my new furry monster

GLOSSARY

Click – minute (30 Earth minutes are 20 intergalactic clicks)

Farstride – satyr unit, approx. 236 metres

Faunus – planet of the satyr

Krat – Satyr expletive

Peritan – human

Peritus – intergalactic term for planet Earth

Rotation – one year in Intergalactic Standard

1 SILUS

It was my turn to watch the Trials. I hated every moment of sitting in my cabin, staring at the screen, watching as contestants were torn apart by beasts or by each other. We were taking turns to avoid becoming desensitised to the violence. None of us were good people. We'd done bad things. Committed crimes. There was a reason why we were in this part of the galaxy, where outlaws were the norm and the Intergalactic Authority had little power. But I had rules; I had limits. There were some things I wouldn't do. I'd not lost my soul quite yet. Stained it, tarnished it, yes, but it was still there. Tattered and curled up in the darkness of all the things I'd done.

Before the events of the past week, I'd never watched the Trials. I'd known how to access them, of course, but I'd always had a bad feeling about them. Watching contestants fight to the death, perish in the harsh jungles of Kalumbu, eaten alive by beasts bred to be always hungry - it wasn't for me.

I clenched my teeth and chose the Trials channel. It was on a hidden frequency that could only be accessed by those who knew what they were doing. A new episode had just begun. The Trials were streaming all day, every day, but some of the episodes were repeats, showing the bloodiest battles and the most horrific deaths in a loop. We weren't interested in those. It gave us some breaks in between watching the Trials, and it meant every crew member only had to spend an IG hour a day in front of our screens.

I should have brought snacks, but yesterday's episode had turned my stomach. I wondered if any of the contestants had volunteered to take part, or if they were all victims, abducted from their homes or spaceships, and forced to fight for the entertainment of others. I wished we could rescue them all. Destroy the Trials once and for all. But that was too dangerous. There was a multi-trillion industry behind the Trials of Kalumbu. Powerful people watched the games, sponsored contestants, bet on them. We'd become even bigger targets if we ended the games. Rescuing a few contestants would hopefully be enough to make a difference without turning ourselves into martyrs.

The first two contestants presented to the audience were males, one Pletorian and one battle-scarred Kardarian, but the third made me clutch my horns. A female, and a Peritan at that.

Breathless, I watched as she blinked into the camera, blinded by the bright lights around her. She was naked, vulnerable, and shivering with fear. I touched the screen before I realised what I was doing. The image froze right when the camera had zoomed in, focusing on the female's face.

Her skin was the colour of my fur, exactly the same shades of brown. Her eyes were a warm amber, framed by long lashes. Her hair had been shaved, either by the game makers or someone else. She had a silver ring in one nostril which seemed to sparkle in the bright lights. She was clearly scared, her lips quivering, her eyes wide, but she stood straight, facing whatever was to come with fire in her eyes.

Something about her felt familiar. The longer I stared at her, the more I felt it.

But it couldn't be.

I forced myself to resume the broadcast, averting my eyes out of respect when the cameras zoomed in on her naked body. Perverts, all of them. There was no reason not to give her clothes. They wouldn't offer her any protection from the dangers of Kalumbu, but at least she'd have her dignity. Even coming from a species that only put on a loincloth when in contact with aliens, I knew that Peritans treasured being covered. Penny had explained it to me when she'd first arrived on the Artep. And the game makers had to know it. It was yet another way of how they manipulated their contestants, making them feel vulnerable before they even set foot on Kalumbu.

Kalumbu, the planet of death. Only two people had ever survived the Trials and they were on board the Artep just now. Other contestants had won the Trials, which was achieved after staying alive for ten days, but we'd discovered quickly that their supposed success didn't last long. They were killed as soon as the cameras were turned off. Nobody had left Kalumbu alive until Fay and Vruhag.

The game makers had already tightened their security since I'd hacked their systems. Rescuing the female wouldn't be as easy as it had been with the orc and his mate. I'd have to find another way to break through the shields they kept around the planet, preventing anyone from flying to the surface or beaming them up into orbit. It had worked last time because they hadn't expected anyone to try.

I focused back on the screen. Raucous applause sounded when the platform the female stood on began to move. She was about to be transported down onto the surface of Kalumbu. She wouldn't last long there. Fay had help from a native species, but what were the chances that the same would happen for this female? No, it was on me to get her out. I had to find a way to hack the systems and fast. Every click that passed could be the one that brought her death.

The camera focused on her face again. All traces of fear had vanished, leaving only cold determination. She seemed to look right at me, her amber eyes dark with defiance, and that's when I knew.

My hearts skipped a beat.

She was mine.

My atm. My mate.

The world seemed to hold its breath. My mate was about to be sent to Kalumbu. I had to save her, no matter the cost. This was no longer just a rescue mission for a random female.

She meant the universe to me.

"I swear on the Horned God that I will save you or die trying," I whispered and pricked my thumbs with my teeth. I smeared the blood over my horns, sealing the oath.

I stared into her amber eyes. "I will come for you."

2 PRIA

I was living a nightmare, but I knew I was wide awake. The noise and smells around me were real. The cool draught pressing against my bare skin was real. The fear I battled was worse than any night terror.

When my small metal cell had started shaking as if racked by an earthquake, I'd felt hope for the first time in weeks. Maybe one of the walls would collapse, giving me a chance of escape. Or the rubble would bury me, ending my miserable life. After at least a month in my dark prison, hope was a ray of light that gave me the energy to stand and face whatever was about to happen.

The walls and ceiling had indeed disappeared, pulling away to the sides until only the floor was left. I'd watched open-mouthed as an invisible giant dismantled my cell. Bright lights glared from all around me, making it impossible to see what lay beyond the metal square I stood on. My knees threatened to give in, but I grit my teeth and stared into the light. I'd survived weeks of starvation, sensory deprivation and torture. I wouldn't give my unseen captors the satisfaction of seeing me crumble now.

A loud voice boomed from all around me, making guttural sounds that didn't sound like any language I was familiar with. He – if it was a male – sounded excited.

I fought the urge to cover my nakedness and forced myself to stand up straight. I raised my chin defiantly and waited for whatever cruel torture they had in store for me.

The voice continued grunting enthusiastically, followed by occasional jeers and claps from what sounded like a large crowd. Was I surrounded by people or was this just a sound effect to scare me? By now, I'd learned not to trust my senses. My captors had proven that they could mess with my perception. Once, I'd woken up to a foot of water in my cell, rising fast until it had reached my neck. A moment later, it had vanished, leaving me completely dry, as if there hadn't been any water at all. They loved messing with me. Were they testing my reactions or did they just like seeing me suffer?

They loved to hurt me. I'd survived more pain than I thought I could endure. They'd humiliated me, shaved off my hair, taken away my clothes. But for some reason, they hadn't broken me. I was still in there, in this naked, defenseless body. They hadn't broken me and they wouldn't succeed today.

The floor started shaking again. I lifted my arms to keep my balance. I half expected the floor to dissolve beneath me, but instead it moved downwards, propelled by invisible forces. It felt like standing in a lift, a lift that accelerated so much that I stumbled to my knees. The forces of gravity pushed me onto the floor until I was flattened against the cold surface. A heavy weight pressed against me, so strong that it would squash me any moment... And still the bright lights blinded me from all sides, hiding my surroundings. I squeezed my eyes shut and focused on breathing. My ribs ached as the pressure intensified, everything hurt. Something wet touched my lip; blood running from my nose. Stars flashed in front of my closed eyes before I succumbed to the darkness.

The gentle melody of birdsong woke me, a lullaby of sorts. The birds were singing peacefully, not alarmed by my presence. I blinked open my eyes, expecting blue sky, but above me was a sea of purple. Huge trees with bark the colour of ripe plum grew so high that I couldn't see the sky past their foliage. Their leaves were shades of violet, wine, mauve, with flashes of bright magenta closer to the ground. I'd never seen anything like it. Where the tree trunks met the earth, they were as wide as a bus, some even bigger.

I sat up slowly, rubbing my eyes. By now, I was used to the unexpected. I'd come to understand that I may no longer be on Earth, among humans. It had taken me weeks to even consider it, but now, sitting beneath purple trees and listening to unfamiliar, exotic birdsong solidified the truth: I was on an alien planet.

I breathed in deep. The air smelled strange, but not unpleasant. Floral yet spicy, with hints of cardamom and cumin. The air was heavy with moisture and for a moment, I was transported back into my nan's kitchen, a huge pot of curry on the stove, her kind eyes smiling down at me. A new call disrupted the birds' melody and I was ripped from the memory. Another bird, or maybe a small animal, sounding panicked. The birds picked up the alarm, their song turning into a wild cacophony.

There was no time to get my bearings. I didn't know where I was, or why I was here, but instinct told me to run. Whatever the birds were warning of could be dangerous. Maybe one of the beings who'd tortured me. I doubted they'd set me free simply to recapture me immediately, but I wouldn't take any chances.

I scrambled up and searched for a path through the purple forest. The undergrowth was thick with roots, branches and dead leaves. Above me, birds were lifting from the trees and all flew into the same direction. The best option would be to follow them. They knew what they were fleeing from. Until I found out what threats were lurking in this strange world, I'd use them as my guides.

My bare feet ached after only a few steps on the rough ground. In my cell, it hadn't mattered much that they'd taken my shoes and clothes, but right now I would have given anything for some boots. Fear drove me on, even when cuts covered my feet and legs. I had to get away. I couldn't run, the thicket was too dense for that, but I walked as fast as I could, bending branches out of the way and climbing over slippery roots. And still, the birds were calling out the alarm.

I kept listening for the sounds of predators, a roar maybe, or a crushing of branches and leaves, but the only thing I could hear were the panicked birds. Maybe I was overreacting, but primal instinct drove me on. I hadn't survived weeks of confinement and torture only to be eaten by an alien beast now.

The soles of my feet were wet with blood and mud. I wouldn't be able to keep going for much longer. I was no longer as physically fit as I had been before I'd woken up in my cell. I'd tried my best to do my daily yoga exercises, but on some days, I'd been in too much pain to get off my bed. I didn't remember most of what they'd done to me, only that it hurt and that it sapped all my strength. Back home, running for half an hour wouldn't have been a problem for me. Now, even walking quickly through the thick undergrowth was making me wheeze. All I wanted was to sit down and rest, but the birds were still flying away from the direction I'd been coming from. Something was out there. Something dangerous.

I got slower and slower, but I kept stumbling along, ignoring the agony in my feet and the ache in my lungs. If the predator liked human blood, it would be able to follow me easily. I was leaving a bloody trail on the ground, but it couldn't be helped. A root caught around my ankle and I tripped, falling face down onto the decaying purple leaves that covered the muddy ground. Exhausted, I just lay there for a moment, too tired to get back on my feet. Suddenly, the noise around me stopped. The birds no longer sang. They no longer flew, their wings rustling the leaves. There was a just a dead, menacing silence.

As quietly as I could, I rolled onto my back to look up at the trees. It was incredible just how high they reached. They seemed to grow all the way into the clouds like mountains.

A shadow moved high above me, something huge. It didn't make a sound. With the size of it, there should have been some sort of noise, even just the creaking of branches, but it was eerily silent. The beast was a black shadow on six spindly legs that wrapped around tree trunks as it made its way through the forest. It had to be at least fifty metres above me, but it was so large that it wouldn't take it long to reach the ground. It reminded me of a crab, but nimbler and far more evil. This beast was stalking prey, following a scent or trace. As it passed over me, its shadow blocked out all light. I shivered from fear and cold. For a tiny moment, it stilled when it was right above me, as if it had noticed my presence, but then it continued moving through the trees. I didn't dare to breathe, let alone move. I stayed on the ground for a few more minutes, praying that the danger had passed. Only when a solitary bird started picking up its song again did I slowly sit up. My vision blurred for a moment. When had I last eaten something?

I had to find food, water and shelter. I didn't know why I was here or for how long they'd let me run free, but I had to plan for every eventuality. In normal life, I liked to take things as they came, trusting for everything to turn out well in the end, but this wasn't a normal situation. This was survival.

3 SILUS

My fist slammed into the wall, leaving a dent. Captain Twim would bill me for the damage. I didn't care. Right now that bastard should be glad I hadn't punched him. I'd come to him expecting his full support. A rescue mission for my mate. But he'd refused. He didn't want to send anyone to the planet's surface. He wanted to watch and observe, gather more data, spend some time hacking their systems. By then, my mate might be dead.

Kalumbu was one of the most hostile planets in this part of the galaxy. Predators roamed the endless forests, while other Trials contestants were only too happy to kill off their competitors. Sometimes, the game masters dropped all the contestants in the same area to watch them fight each other. They believed that the strongest won the Trials and was showered in riches. Ever since we'd rescued two of the contestants, the orc, Vruhag, and his Peritan mate, Fay, we knew that this was a lie. Those who somehow survived the Trials were killed off-camera. Ten planetary rotations, that's how long each Trial was, a little over twelve IG days. Thousands of warriors were dropped onto Kalumbu, each believing that they could make it out alive if only they were smarter, stronger, more ruthless than everybody else. Although not all of them were there voluntarily. That was another lie. Both Vruhag and Fay had been abducted and forced to be in the Trials. Just like my mate. A female from a planet so underdeveloped that they didn't even know other species existed in the universe. I didn't know where Peritus was located, but from what Fay had said, it had many hundreds of generations to go until it would catch up with my own home world. Faunus had been part of the intergalactic community for so long that our people were founding members of many of its institutions, like the Intergalactic University. Space travel was as normal for us satyrs as breathing, yet I'd had enough contact with other species to imagine what it was like to be less advanced.

How had my mate come to Kalumbu? Had she been abducted from the same place as Fay? Who had taken her and why? Was it just for entertainment purposes or was there another reason to target Peritans? From what I'd read about them, they weren't special in any way. On the contrary, they were weak with their hornless, naked bodies. Prey rather than predators.

That said, my mate had shown great strength when she'd stared into the camera full of defiance. She wasn't going to give up. And neither was I.

I hurried to my quarters and packed my things. If Twim wasn't going to help me, then I'd have to rescue her myself. I'd do whatever it took.

All weapons were under strict lock and key on board the Artep, but I was the best hacker, not just on this ship, but in this quadrant. Twim's cheap security proved no match to me, so I helped myself to as many guns and knives as I could carry. A spear caught my eye when I left the weapon storage. I remembered taking it from an enemy raider a few months ago. At my touch, the spear shortened into a silver rod about the length of my forearm. I found a holster forgotten in a corner and wrapped it around my waist. I'd watched enough of the Trials to know that some of the beasts down there were impervious to modern guns. The spear might come in useful.

I checked my commband to avoid any of my fellow crew members as I made my way to the shuttle bay. I didn't want to have to explain why I was dressed for battle. I wasn't close enough with any of them to make them go against Twim's orders. For the first time since joining his ragtag crew, I regretted not spending more time socialising.

Both shuttles were parked in the hangar, both looking similarly in need of repairs. We'd recently taken in two refugees from the Kalumbu space station, a huge Gofren named Qong and his Peritan mate, Penny, who had immediately started upgrading the Artep. She'd spent years as a slave on the station, repairing its sewers, and was desperate to show Twim that it had been worth taking the two of them on board.

It was strange how I'd never met a Peritan until Penny had turned up, and now I knew two and was about to search for a third. My mate. This peculiar species certainly liked to appear in swarms. If my mate was anywhere near as kind and clever as Penny and Fay, I'd be a very happy male.

A quick scroll through the data on my commband showed me that the shuttle on the left, the Razor, had the fuller tank. Even though I could see on my device that I was alone in the shuttle bay, I looked around me several times while hurrying to the ship. Just like the Artep, it looked like a rusty fossil from the outside, but inside the technology was surprisingly new. Captain Twim didn't care about appearances, only about performance. It was one of the reasons I'd joined his crew.

After this, if I made it back alive, I'd likely have to find myself a new job. I was going against his direct orders. Not that I cared. I'd travel through a black hole if it helped save my mate.

The shuttle smelled of oil and sweat. I didn't want to know who had flown her last. Not everyone on Twim's crew had an understanding of decent bodily hygiene.

I went through the pre-flight checks automatically, then paused for just a moment. As soon as I unlocked the hangar doors, Twim would know what I'd done. There'd be no way back.

It didn't matter. I had to get to Kalumbu.

Ignoring the tension in my horns, I entered the code that would open the air lock. The huge double doors opened frustratingly slowly. As soon as the opening was wide enough for the Razor to squeeze through, I started the shuttle and hit the accelerator. There was no time to lose.

When I'd reached a safe distance from the Artep, I engaged the autopilot so that I could focus on Kalumbu's defences. The entire planet was shielded against incoming traffic. I'd hacked their system once before, when we'd rescued Vruhag and Fay, but I was sure they'd since plugged the holes in their security that I had exploited. At the thought of how Twim had agreed to save those two but not my mate, a growl broke from my chest. Why was my mate worth less? She might not be a battle-hardened orc, but she might have other skills that Twim could exploit. He was a shrewd Mondian, always looking to profit from any given situation. He hadn't organised their rescue out of the goodness of his heart – or did Mondians have several hearts? I couldn't remember.

A beep alerted me of an incoming transmission. I didn't have to look at the screen to know that it was Twim. I ignored him. I didn't have the time to deal with his anger. I'd reach the first invisible barrier shortly and still hadn't cracked Kalumbu's security.

I was a good hacker. No, an excellent hacker. I could break into any system given the time. But I didn't have time. My mate was on the planet's surface. She may already be fighting for her life. I didn't want to think of the alternative. She couldn't be dead. I would have felt it. Right? We were mates. I couldn't believe that I wouldn't feel her death somehow.

My horns ached at the thought. She was alive. Had to be. And I'd rescue her. I'd get us both far away from Kalumbu.

Another beep. Again, I ignored it. A click later, my commband vibrated. I couldn't resist a peek.

>>*If they catch you, you're on your own.*<<

I snarled at Twim's message. He was distracting me and for what? I already knew that he wouldn't risk his own arse. He could go krat himself.

I turned back to my screen and sieved through the code as fast as I could. The first barrier was getting ever closer. If I didn't find a way to break through the firewalls in the next few clicks, I'd have to change course, which would waste valuable time.

They'd fixed every single loophole I'd found the last time. I had to give it to them, they'd acted quickly. I'd underestimated them. Kalumbu itself was a feral, hostile planet, but the people in charge knew what they were doing. This was a trillion credits industry. Every death likely made the game makers more money than I'd seen in my lifetime. They'd protect their investment, no matter the cost.

A yellow light flashed, alerting me of the barrier. Once it turned red, I'd have to turn around. Krat.

I scrolled through the code, trying to spot a gap in the security. Nothing. With more time, I could have written what I liked to call a needle-ram, a tiny weapon that expanded once it embedded itself in the code, but time was the one thing I didn't have. With every click that passed, my mate came closer to death.

Suddenly, a line of code turned bright blue. As I watched, some of the symbols changed. Someone was working on Kalumbu's security from the other side. That could be my chance. I typed furiously, trying to find a way to exploit that change.

Another line shifted.

>>xs8f0ajfhofa *You are welcome* ja9000a=fgagjx[<<

I stared at the embedded message. A moment later, the yellow light stopped flashing. I switched screens and checked the status of the barrier. It was open. I double checked it, triple checked, then hit the accelerator.

A tiny voice in my mind warned me that it could be a trap, but I ignored it. I had to get to my mate. If a mysterious stranger wanted to help me, so be it. And if it was a trap, we'd find a way out of it. Together, once I had my mate in my arms. My hearts beat a little faster at the thought of holding her. It's what I'd been waiting for all my life. This was not how I'd imagined meeting my mate for the first time, but I thanked the gods nonetheless for leading me here.

As soon as I was through the barrier, the yellow light came on again. I was locked in. I'd figure out how to get out later.

For now, I turned on the Trials of Kalumbu channel and instructed the shuttle's AI to locate my mate.

I was coming for her.

4 PRIA

t was getting dark and I still hadn't found food, water or shelter. I'd hoped for a stream, some berries, a cave, but there was nothing but trees, dead wood and thorny bushes. I dragged myself along, stumbling so often that my legs would be covered in bruises by tomorrow, hoping that this nightmare would end. I didn't dare look at my feet. They felt as if my skin was in tatters. It was a miracle no predator had caught the scent of my blood yet. Above me, the birds were getting quieter as the light waned. The foliage was too thick to see the sun, but the shadows had been growing longer for hours now. I didn't have high hopes of surviving this place once night fell. If the monsters hunting during the day were as huge and creepy as that tree-crab, I didn't want to know what the nocturnal beasts looked like.

I was so fucked.

I cringed at the mental curse, almost feeling my nan boxing my ears. I didn't usually use such language, not even in my thoughts, but this was an unusual situation. Today, I'd been in a prison cell that had then turned into a lift so fast I'd fallen unconscious, woken up on an alien planet and encountered a horrifying monster. Yes, I was allowed to curse as much as I wanted to.

A bird's screech from high above was the only warning I got. Something moved to my right, a shadow jumping from behind a bush. I took a step back, but a root caught around my ankle and I slipped on the muddy ground. That probably saved my life. A spear grazed the top of my head even as I fell. A sharp pain on my scalp made me wince, but it was nowhere near as bad as the agony in my feet and legs.

My attacker stepped into a solitary ray of light piercing through the leaves, revealing the creature in all its ugliness. Dark grey fur covered its entire body, matted and streaked with dirt. It had two legs that were vaguely humanoid, but its torso was strangely elongated, ending in a flurry of tentacles on which a bulbous head throned. One of the tentacles held another spear, already pointing at me. The creatures four eyes flashed with intelligence. A sentient being. An alien. Oh wow, this was my first face-to-face encounter with an alien. The torture in my cell had been conducted in total darkness; I'd never actually seen my jailors. I'd imagined them as human first, until they'd touched me and I'd felt their sticky, cold skin on mine.

The alien moved its tentacle, ready to throw that spear.

"Wait!" I shouted before I knew what I was doing. "Don't!"

It stared at me with unblinking white eyes. Creepy. For a moment, I hoped that it would change its mind now that it knew I was sentient, that I wasn't just an animal it could kill for food, but then it aimed at me again.

I rolled to my right as fast as I could to avoid the spear. Through some miracle, it hit the ground next to me, followed by an angry hiss from the alien. Now both its spears were gone, but it still looked dangerous even without weapons. I bet those tentacles could strangle me if I let it get too close.

I didn't know what possessed me to pick up the closest spear. I'd never handled any kind of weapon before, let alone an archaic looking spear. It was heavier than it looked. The wooden shaft was rough and uneven, but holding it instantly made me feel a little safer.

Stumbling to my feet, I used the spear for support before lifting it, pointing the sharpened end at the alien. It hissed, its tentacles swirling menacingly all around its upper body.

"I don't want to hurt you," I said as loudly and confidently as I could, even though I felt like my legs were about to give way. "Go away and I will let you leave."

Of course, it didn't know what I was saying. It snarled again, exposing rows of tiny sharp teeth in a mouth that was too big for its head. I shuddered. This was a creature of nightmares.

I waved the spear at it, hoping I looked menacing enough to get the message across. I wouldn't hesitate to defend myself. I may have looked a lot weaker than this alien, naked and injured as I was, but my will to survive was powerful.

Finally, he hissed one last time and then turned, running off into the gloomy forest. I waited until he was completely out of sight before I let myself sag against the nearest tree. I needed to find somewhere I could rest in relative safety. It was already getting hard to see and full darkness would be upon me way too soon. This encounter had wasted valuable time.

I picked up the second spear and continued in the same direction I'd been heading, using the spears as walking sticks. They were heavy, but at least they stopped me from tripping as often as I had before.

When it got too dark to see, I swept one of them in front of me to feel for obstacles. Stopping here felt like a bad idea, so I continued on, slowly but steady. I didn't know what I was looking for, what I expected to find in the dark, but somehow, I found the energy to press on. Listening to my instincts had been beneficial so far; hopefully it would stay that way.

I squealed when my right foot hit something wet. For a moment, I hoped I'd stepped into a stream, but I couldn't hear any running water. And it was too warm. The liquid I stood in was the temperature of a hot bath, comforting yet also disconcerting. Hot springs would make a sound, right? So what was this? Without a torch or even moonlight to illuminate my surroundings, I couldn't be sure. I hit the ground around me with one of the spears. Right in front of me, it touched something soft. A horrifying squelch echoed through the quiet forest, followed by a rancid smell that made me cough.

Please don't be a dead body. Don't be a flesh-eating plant. Don't be some sort of alien trap.

I decided I didn't really want to know. I turned to my right and hurried away as fast as I could until I could no longer smell that stench.

Something hard hit my cheek. A branch? I touched my skin only to feel wetness running down my face. I was bleeding from yet another place. Great. If I somehow made it through this night alive, it would be a miracle.

After another ten minutes or so of struggling along, I picked up an entirely new sound. A distant rumble, like from an engine. Were these my jailors coming to take me back? I turned away from the sound when the rumbling sputtered. A flash of light lit up the forest, followed by a loud crash. Above me, birds chittered in alarm and leaves rustled as unseen creatures moved. Then, silence.

Now I had a choice. Head as far away from whatever had crashed or walk towards it. Maybe it was another human sent on one of those lift things. Maybe my own cell-turned-lift had made the same noise. If there was even the tiniest chance that someone else was out there, a human, who could help me, or was in need of help... I had to try.

I grit my teeth and stumbled through the darkness.

The smell of smoke was growing so strong that my nose stung and my eyes teared up. Flames flickered behind some gigantic trees. I was close enough now to hear the crackling of the fire. Hopefully, it wouldn't spread and burn down the forest. Surviving a wildfire wasn't on my list for this night.

I walked around a tree trunk as wide as an entire house and the crash site finally came into view. Something big had gone down here, a twisted metal object surrounded by hungry flames. Definitely not of human origin.

I should run.

But something made me linger. Curiosity, maybe, or something deeper. A strange sense of importance filled me. I had to be here, in this place, in this moment.

So I took another step towards the crash site. And another.

Something moved among the flames. I gripped my spears a little tighter. I should run. I really, really should run.

A man walked through the fire, just a shadow in the smoke. Two legs, two arms, too tall and bulky to be a woman. A human man. Had to be. Maybe it was wishful thinking, maybe I was deluded.

"Hello!" I shouted, but then smoke entered my throat and I coughed.

I waved one of the spears at him.

He turned to me, lifted one hand, and in that moment, a terrible roar resonated through the forest and something broke through the undergrowth behind me.

5 SILUS

This was not how I'd imagined meeting my mate.

The plan had been to find her, beam her into my shuttle and then get away from Kalumbu as fast as I could. But the Horned God had had other ideas for me. As soon as my AI had located my mate, the proximity alarms had blared to life. I'd scarcely believed my eyes when two missiles showed up on the screen. The barrier hadn't been the game makers' only defence.

I was a good enough pilot, but the shuttle was unwieldy and not made for high-speed chases. It had taken all my skill to evade one of the missiles, but the second had clipped one of the engines.

It was said that the Horned God had a twisted sense of humour. I'd crashed, but I'd not only survived, but had also managed to come down close to my mate. Somehow. I still didn't quite know what had happened.

The smoke was making me woozy. I had to get away from the crash. To my mate.

She stood between two gigantic trees, looking very small yet fierce with her two spears. Satyrs didn't see as well in the dark as other species, but the glow of the fire illuminated her body enough for me to know that she was even more beautiful in real life than she had been on screen.

She raised one spear and shouted something that got lost in the crackle of the flames. I was glad she wasn't unarmed, but she didn't seem to have any other equipment. Not even clothes.

Most of the supplies I'd packed were lost in the wreckage, but I still had one handgun and my folded spear. I had also grabbed the basic survival kit stashed under the pilot seat which hopefully contained some nutrient cubes and water purification tablets. It would also include a beacon, but Twim had made it clear that I couldn't hope for any rescue attempt. The beacon would likely attract the game makers, so I wouldn't risk using it.

A roar echoed through the night. A predator's triumphant warning. Something was close.

I sprinted towards my mate, detaching the spear from its holster as I ran. It unfolded just in time. A quecklra burst from the darkness, a monster I'd seen in the Trials before. They were common on Kalumbu and one of the main causes of death among contestants. Quecklra were long, at least four times as long as I was tall, with flexible bodies that enabled them to weave through the trees. They stood on ten spindly legs tipped with razor-sharp talons. But its biggest weapon were its two poisoned stingers that would immobilise its victims almost immediately. One its prey was defenceless, the quecklra would tear it apart - while the contestant was still alive - before gulping down the body parts. It was not a pretty way to die.

I'd seen a lot of horrible, disgusting things in my life, but watching a quecklra feed on its prey on screen had made me queasy. Now I was facing one in real life. Its gaping maw was so high above us it was hard to see much more than a dark shape, but I knew the stingers were the bigger danger. I racked my brain whether I'd ever seen a contestant kill a quecklra. Yes, once, but that Karpartian had been given a laser sword by a sponsor and managed to cut off the quecklra's legs, leaving it unable to follow him. I doubted my gun would do much against the touch chitin hide of the beast. I could try and gouge out its eyes with my spear, but its head was too far away. I'd have to lure it to lower itself to the ground.

All this flashed through my mind while I ran. When I reached my mate, she was bravely facing the beast. She looked unsteady on her feet, and I could smell the iron scent of her blood, but there was no time to check her for injuries.

The quecklra moved faster than monster of that size should have been able to. Its hind legs lowered as one of the stingers shot out of the darkness, aiming right at my mate. I jumped in front of her, my spear aimed at the stinger. I would have preferred an axe to cleave off that poisonous appendage, but the spear would have to do. When the spear hit the stinger, I barely held on to it. My arms shook at the force of the impact, but I held on, twisting the shaft in the hope of doing as much damage as possible. The quecklra chittered in anger. A movement out of the corner of my eye was all the warning I got. The second stinger, its tip oozing with yellow poison, headed for us. At the same time, my spear was still embedded in the other stinger, even though the quecklra tried hard to dislodge it by whipping it up and down. I was holding on for dear life.

I still had a gun tucked into a holster around my waist, but I needed both hands to grip the spear.

"Take the gun, quickly," I told my mate, not taking my eyes off the stingers.

She didn't question me. Didn't protest, didn't say that she didn't know how the gun worked. She simply pulled it, aimed at the second stinger, and fired.

If I hadn't been sure that this was indeed my gods-given mate, I would have known now. She was utterly perfect.

The laser beam glinted in the dark, but missed the stinger by a hair's width.

"Again," I ordered.

This time, she hit it. I'd almost expected the shot to be reflected by the quecklra's thick chitin hide, but it had to be thinner around the stingers. The quecklra reared back with such force that my spear was pulled from the stinger. I staggered back, dark green blood running down my weapon and onto my hands. It stung, but there was no time to wipe it off.

The quecklra was angry. Furious. It stomped around, making the ground shake, its talons leaving deep imprints in the soft earth. It had learned its lesson, however, and didn't try another attack with its stingers. Instead, it lowered itself down by bending its legs in twisted angles until its slobbering maw was right above us. Just what I'd hoped for. If it got a little closer, I might be able to try and aim at its eyes or spear it through its jaws.

"Duck as low as you can," I warned my female.

I felt her hesitate. I didn't have time to explain my plan to her. If she got in the way, the quecklra might hurt my mate - or worse. There was only one other option. I swung my spear, kicking the legs out from under my female.

"I'm sorry," I mouthed, quickly checking that I hadn't injured her, before turning my full attention back to the monster. Long tendrils of spittle were dripping from its open maw. Endless rows of sharp teeth glinted in the shine of the fire. It would be able to rip me apart with a single bite. I only had one chance.

I tightened the grip on my spear and waited for the right moment. If I threw it too early, it wouldn't hit the beast with enough power. If I waited too long, I might end up dead. Or worse, my mate might be hurt. Any injury on

Kalumbu could mean certain death. Predators were waiting to exploit our weaknesses, as were other contestants. I wouldn't have been surprised if there were beasts lurking in the trees, watching our fight, hoping for an easy meal at the end of it.

They'd have to go hungry.

I raised my spear and sent a silent prayer to the Horned God. Please let it fly true.

"Watch out!" my mate suddenly cried.

Her warning saved my life. I swirled around at the same time as something hard smashed into my lower back. I was thrown forwards, right onto my female. I just about managed to roll to my side before jumping back onto my hooves. I still held the spear, but my grip on it had slipped a little. My back was on fire, an agony unlike any I'd ever felt before, but the urge to protect my mate droned out the pain. I focused on the quecklra and threw the spear.

6 PRIA

The alien's spear struck true. The monster, a beast that even my worst nightmares couldn't have conjured up, buckled and twisted, the spear embedded in one of its creepy eyes. The sound coming from its gaping maw was unearthly, something between a chittering and a roar.

With one last hateful, hungry look at us, it turned on its heel – if those talons could be called heels – and disappeared into the darkness. I released a breath I hadn't realised I'd been holding. Everything had happened so fast. The alien emerging from the flames, the monster, the fight.

At some point during the battle, I'd realised that the alien had a tail. He wasn't human after all. From afar, he looked human enough, but up close it was a very different story. What I'd thought was a helmet were actually horns; two huge, curled horns sprouting from the sides of his head. Back home, I would have assumed they were a prop, some weird goat costume, but here, I didn't doubt for a second that they were real. He was an alien. An alien with horns. His ears weren't human either, too pointy and big. His intense brown eyes were framed by bushy eyebrows, while a perfectly groomed goatee graced his angular chin. His chest was bare except for tufts of hair. Usually, I wasn't a fan of chest hair, but in his case, it only made him even more masculine. He wasn't quite as naked as me, even though the only garment he wore was a leather loincloth around his waist. It would have looked comical in any other circumstance, but not here in the jungle. The flames from the wreck illuminated the scene enough to see that his legs were covered in thick fur, the same maroon colour as his long hair. It looked so soft and fluffy that I was tempted to reach out and run my fingers through it, but I thought better of it. I couldn't be sure yet if he was friend or foe.

My gaze moved further down and I couldn't help but suck in a sharp breath when I saw that his legs ended in hooves rather than feet. That realisation made the pain in my own feet flare up again. I grit my teeth, trying to suppress the urge to wince.

I was still on the ground where the alien had pushed me. That had been a total dick move. I would have ducked. Not that I was used to battling deadly monsters, but I had a good survival instinct.

"I would have ducked," I said aloud, realising the alien was staring at me just like I'd been checking him out. "I would have ducked."

He held out a hand to help me up. "I apologise. I had to make sure."

Ignoring his hand, I sat up a little straighter, but didn't stand. My feet were on fire. I didn't think I'd be able to walk any further tonight.

The alien turned in the direction the monster had disappeared, his ears twitching. He picked up my two spears and stuck them through holes in his belt. His own spear was still embedded in the monster.

"We are safe for now, but we shouldn't linger. The quecklra might return with friends."

"The kwe… what?"

"Quecklra," he repeated more slowly. "One of the most dangerous predators here on Kalumbu. We're lucky to have escaped with our lives."

"Kalumbu? Is that what this place is called? Why are you here? Are you with-"

"No time," he interrupted not unkindly. "We have to go now."

"We? Why should I trust you?"

He turned back to me, his expression dark. "Because I'm the only hope you have of ever leaving this planet alive."

Good enough for me. He didn't feel like a threat. And even if he was, it wasn't as if I could run away. I was a sitting duck, ready to be eaten by the next monster that passed this way. He was my best option.

"I don't think I can walk," I admitted with a nod towards my feet. I didn't want to have a closer look at my shredded legs. Once I saw the damage, I may no longer be able to hold back the tears.

I watched him as his gaze wandered to my feet. His eyes went wide, but my attention was captured by his ears. They curled up, the ends drooping like wilting flowers. I felt strangely sad at the sight.

He said something in another language, harsh words that were clearly curses. "I will make them pay," he muttered in English, "I swear it to you. They will suffer as they made you suffer."

He knelt by my side, his furry knees touching my bare thighs. A jolt of warmth shot through me where we touched. How strange. But certainly not the strangest thing happening to me today, so I ignored it.

"I will carry you," he said. It wasn't a question. He wasn't asking for permission.

I should have protested. Shouldn't let this stranger take control. Instead, I asked, "Where to?"

He tapped the leather brace around his right wrist. A topographic map appeared *in the air above it.* "The shuttle's AI calculated the safest shelter options just before we crashed and sent the data to my commband. The closest one is only six farstrides from here."

Commband? Farstrides? AI? I had so many questions, but before I could ask even a single one, he slipped one arm underneath my knees and another under my arms and lifted me. I was squeezed against his chest – his *bare* chest – while he carried me easily, without a single groan or huff of exhaustion. I tried not to lean my head against his bare skin, but I couldn't help but breathe in his earthy scent. Roasted chestnuts with a hint of thyme. His skin was warm, hotter than it should have been despite the temperate night air. He would be great to keep close if the temperatures fell overnight.

No. I erased that thought from my mind.

All I wanted was to get home alive, in one piece, without more mental scars than I already had.

We continued in silence, both of us listening for threats. The alien seemed to have better night vision than me; he didn't stumble even once. The further we got away from the crash site, the less I could see as the glow of the flames was blocked out by giant trees, until I couldn't even make out the alien's face above me.

The alien. We'd never introduced ourselves to each other. Fighting a nightmarish monster had taken priority.

"I'm Pria," I whispered.

"Pree-ah," he echoed without changing his fast gait. "Beautiful."

I waited for him to tell me his name, but he stayed quiet.

"And you are...?" I tried eventually.

"Silus Longtail."

More silence. I took the hint and kept my mouth shut.

My legs were burning with pain, made worse every time they bumped against a branch, bush or root. Silus clearly tried to find an easy passage through the forest, but the undergrowth was too thick. Several times, he had to turn back and try a different route.

Exhaustion was getting the better of me. I let my head rest against the alien's chest and closed my eyes. The deep drum beat of his heart was a soothing lullaby. Sleep embraced me, carrying me away from the pain-

"We're here."

I groaned softly, frustrated that I didn't get to have a nap. Then I realised I'd been about to fall asleep in the arms of a stranger, and not only that, an alien with horns, hooves and a tail. I couldn't let my guard down. He may seem like a good guy, but it was very possible that he was in league with my captors. What were the chances of a knight in shining fur just happened to crash his spaceship when I needed him? I had to keep my wits about me and be wary of the alien. This could all be part of some twisted experiment. Find out how long the human takes to trust the good cop after being released by the bad cops. Something like that.

Silus gently lowered me to the ground, setting me down on something soft and warm. I couldn't see a thing.

"Where are we?" I asked, keeping my voice low just in case.

"A tree cave. Is there something wrong with your eyes?" He sounded concerned.

"No, but it's pitch black out there. Humans can't see in the dark."

"Oh. They never said."

"They?" I asked sharply. I'd been right! He hadn't just crashed here by accident. It had been part of the plan. I scuffled away from him, ignoring the pain shooting through my feet and legs, but I bumped against something hard almost immediately. Wood. Part of a tree?

"It's a long story. You're not the first Peritan I've met. Now stop moving, you'll injure yourself further. Let me look at your wounds."

He sounded so very calm and reassuring. I wanted to believe that he had my best interests at heart, but after what I'd been through, I couldn't.

"Who are you?" I demanded. "Why are you here?"

"I will answer your questions if you keep still and let me care for your injuries. Deal?"

I should have got up and run, but my feet wouldn't have carried me far. I'd already had a taste of the monsters lurking in this forest. Right now, staying with Silus seemed like the safer option. For now. As soon as the sun rose and my legs hurt a little less, I'd escape. I wouldn't be part of this game. I wouldn't let them manipulate me.

"Deal," I sighed, then winced when he touched the heel of my right foot.

"I'm sorry, I'll be as gentle as I can. Let me see if there are any painkillers in the survival kit." I heard him rummage through something. After a while, he huffed in frustration. "Who the kratting krat packed this? Water purification tablets but no container to collect water. Mood stims but not a single painkiller. Not even disinfectant. At least there are some smart bandages, but I would have liked to clean your wounds first. At first light, I will go and search for water. Until then, I can give you some mood stims to distract you from the pain."

Was he offering me drugs?

"What are they?" I asked.

"They also call them happy pills. They make you forget about your problems."

"Are they drugs? Do they make you addicted?"

He chuckled softly. "Only if you take them every day for a rotation. And I won't let you do that. Open your mouth. They go under your tongue."

I wasn't sure if I wanted this, but then another wave of pain brought tears to my eyes and I opened my mouth. His thumb pressed on my bottom lip. Goosebumps rolled over my skin, a pleasant shiver that ran all the way to my core. What the ever-loving fuck?

He pushed a tiny round pearl into my mouth. As soon as he withdrew his fingers, an overly sweet taste overwhelmed my senses.

"That's too.... ooooh..."

I landed on a fluffy cloud. It wrapped itself around me, holding me in the most comforting hug I could have imagined. I relaxed into the cloud's warm embrace and smiled. Life wasn't all that bad after all.

7 SILUS

She looked so beautiful when she was fully relaxed. Her long lashes were the same colour as my fur. It was a sign. We were meant for each other. For the first time since I'd met her, the folds between her eyebrows smoothed. Her lips curved into a content smile. It had felt so good to touch those lips. For a moment, I'd imagined what it would feel like to have her suck on my finger, what it would feel like to kiss her soft lips. But it wasn't appropriate in this situation. I had to get her to safety first. This was all new to her. The first time she was on another planet, the first time she'd met a different species. I'd keep quiet about us being mates until I was sure she could handle it.

I carefully removed leaves, dirt and debris from her legs and feet, cursing the game makers every time she flinched. Her skin was caked in blood, her skin shredded. I didn't understand how she'd been able to stand. I wished nothing more than to take her pain away and heal her wounds. My mate wasn't supposed to suffer. I'd failed to protect her from this. Maybe if I'd been faster in evading the missiles, if I hadn't lost control of the shuttle, if I'd volunteered to watch more of the Trials and seen her in an earlier episode...

It was no use pondering on what ifs. I had to focus on how to get us off this planet. Captain Twim wouldn't send a rescue party, he'd made that very clear. Would the other two Peritans, Penny and Fay, help us? I was sure they'd try to come to the aid of a fellow Peritan, but they had no ship, no resources to call their own. Maybe if they persuaded their mates, they could do something - but what? I'd barely made it through Kalumbu's security shields. If they realised I'd squeezed through, they may already be working on a fix. I'd had help from that mysterious hacker on the other side, but would that person help a second time? Unlikely. If they'd even helped. Maybe it had all been a trap. Maybe the hacker had sent the missiles that had downed my shuttle. The game makers loved to have sets of mates in the Trial. It was good entertainment to see them suffer together.

Now we were trapped on the surface of Kalumbu. My mate was injured and I'd received bruises and scrapes in the battle. My back still hurt, but it had turned from flaming agony into a dull ache that I was able to ignore. We had only the bare essentials in the survival kit: water purification tablets, smart bandages, a handful of out-of-date nutrient bars, a small pocket knife and an emergency beacon. I clipped the knife to my loincloth. We also had two primitive spears that wouldn't survive more than one fight. I didn't know where my mate had found them, but it was better than nothing. I mourned the loss of my own spear. I hoped the wound would fester and kill that kratting quecklra.

When I gently pulled the last thorn from my mate's toes, I wrapped the smart bandages around her feet and legs. She moaned softly, but her eyes stayed closed. She had to be dreaming. The sound made my cock harden. It had been a good idea to give her the mood stim. Now her wounds were as clean as I could get them without disinfectant or boiled water. I hoped she wouldn't get an infection. I had to get her off this planet and into a medpod as soon as possible. Until then, we had to survive the dangers of Kalumbu. Monsters, flesh-eating plants, and of course other contestants. We didn't stand much of a chance in our current state. At least we'd made it to this tree cave. The entrance was so narrow it had been a squeeze for me to fit through, but inside it was roomy enough to stand upright. Any monster larger than me wouldn't be able to get to us here.

Not that the big ones were the only creatures to fear. I'd seen contestants eaten alive by swarms of bugs as small as the palm of my hand. Until we'd rescued Vruhag and Fay, I'd believed there were no harmless creatures on Kalumbu. They'd told us a fanciful tale of many-tailed fluffy beings that were not only benevolent, but also sentient. A tribe of them had taken the orc and his Peritan mate in and protected them from harm. I still had trouble believing that tale. We'd gone through the footage of the Trials to find evidence of the chii, as they called themselves, but the only proof of their existence was a blurry shot of a golden tail that could have easily belonged to another animal. They were clearly used to hiding from the game makers' camera drones.

If nobody came to rescue us, maybe I should try and find the chii. But how? I didn't even know if they lived in this part of the planet. My mate had been dropped far from where Vruhag and Fay had battled for their lives. I turned on my commband and had it calculate a route to approximately where the den of the chii was located. I almost laughed at the result. We'd have to walk for 412 rotations of the planet. We wouldn't survive that long. No, the chii weren't an option, unless they also lived in this area and somehow made themselves known to us. We were on our own.

Pria's breathing was turning slower as she slipped into deep sleep. I would guard her while she recovered her strength. In the morning, we had to make a decision. Stay here and build a base, or move on to search for a better location. For now, I leaned against the tree's uneven bark and watched my mate as her chest rose and sank in a hypnotic rhythm.

***

A chorus of birds announced the coming of morning long before the first rays of the sun reached our shelter. Pria had slept through the night while I had stood guard. I was tired, but a single night without sleep wouldn't affect my strength. They'd kept us awake for two IG weeks during my military training back on Faunus and still expected us to fight at our best.

I let her sleep for a little longer, watching, admiring, memorising every part of her body. I wish I had a blanket to cover her, or at least a pillow. She was lying naked on the mossy ground, her legs covered in bandages. She looked so very vulnerable, but then I remembered how she'd faced the quecklra with her spears and smiled. She was strong. With a bit of training, she'd be formidable.

She sat up without warning, her eyes wide open.

"Where am I?" She looked straight at me and for a moment, she didn't seem to recognise me. "Oh. So it wasn't a dream."

"No, it wasn't," I said softly. "How are you feeling?"

She stared at her bandaged legs. "Sore. But not as sore as I think I should be."

"The smart bandages encourage healing. It will still take time, but if we're lucky, there won't be any scars."

"Smart bandages," Pria muttered. "Who are you? Where are we? And why can I understand you?"

"I should find us some water and food-"

"No," she interrupted sharply, her dark eyes blazing. "You're going to answer my questions. You had a good excuse for not talking last night, but now you'll tell me everything."

I admired her for standing up to me like that. She was smaller than me, away from her planet for the first time, thrust into a world she didn't understand, but here she was, challenging me. My horns ached with desire. She was my mate, there was no doubt about it. The gods had made us for each other.

"Talk," she demanded. "Now."

I suppressed a smile. "I am Silus from the planet Faunus. My species are called satyr in Intergalactic Standard."

"What's that?"

"A common language processing scheme. It's not so much a language as a way to have a common way of talking about time, distances, species, and so on. Most aliens use the rotation of their planet around their star to define time, for example, but that is useless when they want to talk to other species. That's where Intergalactic Standard comes in. Everyone knows what an IG day is compared to a day on their home planet, so that makes interspecies communication a lot easier. Did that make sense? Sorry, I'm not very good at explaining stuff."

I also wasn't sure I'd said that much in one go ever before. On the Artep, I mostly kept to myself. All of us were outlaws and rogues, but some enjoyed being on the wrong side of the law a lot more than I did. I'd made a mistake and had been made an outcast. It hadn't been my choice to leave Faunus. I wasn't a born space pirate like some of the others.

"I guess that makes sense," Pria said slowly. "So you're an alien. We're on an alien planet. Is this where you're from?"

"No, Faunus is far from here. We're on Kalumbu. It would take too long to explain everything, but what you have to know is that this planet is used as a sort of arena. Contestants are dropped on the surface and then fight to survive. It's called the Trials of Kalumbu."

"I didn't sign up for any trials."

"No, you didn't. Neither did a lot of the others. They pretend everyone's here voluntarily, but that's a lie. The other Peritans… wait, what do you call yourself again? Hu-mun?"

"Human," she corrected. "There are others? Here?" She looked like she was ready to jump up and search for them, so I put a hand on her shoulder to calm her.

"Not here. They're on the Artep, that's the ship I'm – that I was living on." I told her how we'd picked up Penny and her mate Qong at the Kalumbu space station during a refuel stop, and how we'd rescued Fay and Vruhag.

"Are they going to come for us?" Pria asked when I'd finished.

"I don't know," I admitted. "Probably not. Twim, the Artep's captain, made it very clear that I was on my own when I decided to rescue you. But I've already learned that Peritan females are stronger than you look. They might persuade him to send a shuttle. We will see."

I tried to be more optimistic than I felt. Twim was a shrewd Mondian always out for profit. The Peritans had nothing to offer him in return for a rescue mission.

A loud bird's call from outside reminded me that it was time to go. I got to my hooves and grabbed one of the spears, giving the other to Pria.

"I won't be gone long. Stay here. Stay quiet. I'll try to find some rocks or branches to hide the opening. Rest while you can."

"Wait, you still haven't explained how I understand you. And why you're here. And who you are."

It was hard to turn away from her. I would have loved to stay with my mate, answer her questions, get to know her. But we needed water and food. We could talk later, when it got too dark to forage.

"They must have fitted you with a translator implant," I said brusquely while ducking through the gap in the bark. "I will be back soon."

I ripped a few lianas from a nearby branch and arranged them in front of the hollow tree's opening. I could smell my mate's scent from out here. Hopefully, no predators would find her. I had to hurry.

According to my commband, a second possible shelter location was only ten IG clicks from here. I couldn't hear any running water from where I stood, so heading towards that shelter seemed as good a plan as any. Hopefully, I'd find a stream and some edible plants on the way. And if that shelter turned out to be better, I'd carry my mate to it afterwards.

8 PRIA

My mind was swirling with unasked questions and impatience. Silus had been gone for maybe half an hour. How long until he returned?

Hearing about the other two human women had made me decide to stay with him for a while longer. I had to meet them. Maybe we'd find a way home together. Silus was my link to them, whether I could trust him or not. Once he got back, I'd ask him more about the women.

Knowing that one of them had survived staying on this planet was reassuring. If she'd done it, so could I. My feet and legs already felt a lot better. I'd slept through the night despite my injuries, and despite being in a hollow tree with a stranger. The drugs he'd given me must have helped with that. I remembered the blissful feeling of floating on clouds. I wanted to feel that peace again rather than my current agitation.

The sounds coming from outside weren't calming. Birds screeching in alarm, branches cracking, other beasts calling in the distance. Silus had put something over the opening in the tree, making it even darker inside, but I was sure any determined predator would get to me if it caught my scent. At least my legs weren't bleeding any longer. I just had to stay quiet and wait.

Easier said than done. I was bored. How was it possible to be bored while in mortal peril on an alien planet? It boggled my mind, but it didn't make that restless feeling go away.

I missed having a watch to see time pass. Scratch that, I missed having clothes. It was warm enough that I didn't feel cold, but even without anyone to see me, I felt vulnerable and exposed. Strange how it hadn't felt that way earlier with Silus. I'd not felt embarrassed in his presence, even though he'd been able to see *everything*. He'd looked like he'd stayed up all night; enough time to check out every part of my body. But I didn't feel threatened by him. On the contrary, I'd felt safe. I wanted him back because I wanted to feel that way again. Safe and protected.

He hadn't touched me except for when he'd put one large hand on my shoulder. His skin had been hard and calloused. I'd wanted him to keep his hand there. I'd wanted him to touch me in other places. It had taken a lot of self-control not to react to that desire.

I stared into the gloomy tree cave, counting the roots dangling above me. Just like the bark, they were a deep purple. So very alien. It was hard to know what time it was. How long had Silus been gone now? When should I start to get worried?

I hated inaction. I wasn't someone who sat around and waited for something to happen. I was a go-getter with very little patience. It was one of the reasons why I'd taken up yoga and meditation. It had helped calm my mind, but it hadn't taken away the impatience that sometimes got me in trouble. Waiting was agony. There was nothing for me to do. For a moment, I considered practising with the spear, but the tree cave was too small. I'd likely injure myself trying to kill some imaginary foes. Besides, something told me that they wouldn't stay imaginary for much longer.

Kalumbu. I whispered the word, the alien name of this place. It didn't sound as threatening and deadly as Silus had described the planet. But our encounter with that kweck-monster last night had proved beyond doubt that Kalumbu was dangerous. I shouldn't go outside. I really, really shouldn't. But I had to pee.

The moment I realised that, my bladder seemed to be close to bursting. I had to relieve myself and I certainly wouldn't do it in here, in the cave we might spend another night in.

I checked that the bandages were still tightly wrapped around my feet and legs before I slowly stood up. The soles of my feet ached, but it was nothing like the pain I'd endured yesterday. The bandages felt thicker than socks, giving me enough protection to walk without fear of yet more injuries. I took two wobbling steps to the tree cave's entrance. A few thick, purple branches hung in my way. They were heavier than they looked and it took all my strength to push them aside. Silus had needed to duck to exit the cave, but I was just about able to walk through. One twig snapped out of my grip and banged against my head.

I couldn't suppress a cry of pain. Immediately, the birds all around me fell silent. Well, shit. I'd drawn attention to myself before I'd even left the shelter. I better hurry up.

I hobbled a few steps to a golden bush sprouting aquamarine flowers and squatted behind it. My hands automatically wandered to my waist to open my jeans before I realised that I didn't wear any clothes. As much as I hated being naked, it did make some things easier.

By the time I was done, the birds had started singing again. I looked up, but couldn't see any of them. The foliage was so thick that they had plenty of places to hide, but I was sure that they had their eyes on me. Turning back to the tree cave, I shuddered at the thought of going back inside. Out here, it was lovely. A few rays of sunshine broke through the trees. Dust danced within them, tiny sparkles that seemed like magic glitter. The chorus of the birds was a soothing, hypnotising melody. I wanted to lie down and simply listen while the sun warmed my naked body. The cave was gloomy and cold. I had no desire to go back in. Maybe I could sit near the opening. If a predator came, I could always retreat inside. Yes, that was a good idea.

I limped to the huge purple tree that housed our cave and looked up the trunk. It reached so far into the sky that I couldn't see where it ended. Trees like that shouldn't be possible, but on this planet, they were. Just like monsters that even my wildest nightmares couldn't have conjured. I shuddered at the memory of yesterday's attack. Hopefully, those kind of monsters only came out at dusk.

Standing was getting painful. I sat down against the tree trunk, the soft moss beneath me almost as comfortable as my sofa back home. The bark was warm against my bare skin. It wasn't as rough as it had looked and seemed to give in a little when I pressed my back against it. The birdsong around me was getting calmer, as if the birds were getting tired. I closed my eyes and breathed in the warm forest air. This was lovely. Not at all like the dangerous forest from last night. This was an inviting, warm, gentle forest that I could enjoy without fear. I smiled. So comfy.

So tired.

The birds' lullaby cradled me and rocked me to sleep.

I knew I was dreaming right away. I was back home, in my kitchen, but I wasn't alone as usual. Someone stood by the window, their back turned to me. Sunlight streamed through the dusty glass, turning them into a dark silhouette. I blinked, trying to discern who was in the room with me. A deep sense of unease made me get up from my kitchen chair. The other person didn't move, didn't react at all. Were they even breathing?

Unease turned to fear. They shouldn't be here. Not in my kitchen, not in my dream.

I had to get rid of them.

Suddenly, I had a knife in my hand. I didn't question it. This was a dream. Things didn't always happen in a logical order.

I pointed the knife at the person. "Leave."

They didn't react.

"Leave now," I commanded. My voice trembled ever so slightly.

This was wrong. It was my dream, I was supposed to be in command here. This person felt like a foreign presence that was in my dream, but not part of it. A parasite.

"Leave!" I shouted, brandishing my knife.

Slowly, the figure turned around. The sun blinded me and I looked at the floor, but not before I'd seen two red eyes staring at me.

A hiss made me freeze with fear. Cold shivers cascaded down my back. I wanted to run, but I couldn't move. My feet were glued to the floor and I had no chance but to stare at the dark shape in front of me. Something touched my chin, an invisible finger that forced me to look up, right into the red eyes.

I saw nothing but red. Fire, blood, rage.

The hissing grew louder, echoing all around the room. Something was coming, something even worse than this merciless sea of angry red. I had to run. Had to get away before it was too late.

But I couldn't move.

Couldn't even turn around when I heard the door creak open behind me.

Something slithered into the room. I wanted to scream, but my lips were glued together. I stared into the unblinking red eyes as the knife dropped from my hand.

9 SILUS

The second shelter was a hole in the ground. I cursed the AI that had given me hope of a proper hideout. This was even worse than the tree cave. At least I'd found a muddy stream on the way here. I'd drank my fill, but without anything to carry water, I'd memorised the location so that I could carry my mate here later. I kept looking for something I could use as a bottle, a hollow fruit maybe or a leaf sturdy enough to fashion into a sack, but so far, I'd been unsuccessful. This entire expedition had been a waste of time. I hadn't found food, the shelter had turned out to be no shelter at all, and more time had passed than I'd anticipated. The undergrowth was thick and I'd had to double back several times to find a path through the forest.

I felt like a disappointment. I wasn't providing for my mate. I was letting her down. I had to up my game if we were to survive Kalumbu. Starting with returning to her as fast as possible so she could get some water. She'd been on the planet for even longer and who knew how she'd been treated beforehand. If what Vruhag had said about his captivity was anything to go by, she'd be malnourished and dehydrated.

I didn't know enough about Peritans to know if she was too thin or not. She didn't look like she was about to keel over from starvation, but who was I to know. Once we got off this kratting planet, I'd do my research. I'd treat her like a queen. Like an empress. No, a goddess. She deserved it.

On the way back to the tree cave, I spotted a bush of small golden berries that looked edible. I grabbed a handful, planning to test them once I was with my mate. If they turned out to be digestible and non-poisonous, I'd get more. I'd watched too many episodes of the Trials to get my hopes up. Most plants on Kalumbu were deadly for contestants. The local animals had evolved to be immune to their flora's toxins, but not us. At least half of all Trials contestants died from poisonous plants or starvation, although not many of those deaths made it into the live coverage. They weren't entertaining enough unless it was a particularly slow and painful ending.

My hearts beat rapidly when our tree came into view. I couldn't wait to see my mate again. Breathe in her tantalising scent. Carrying her had been torture. I'd wanted to taste her the entire time. I couldn't wait to claim her. And get to know her properly. Not necessarily in that order. Mating was always different for females. They needed more time. Their physical drive wasn't as strong for them. Controlling their mating urges was a challenge for males, one that proved to their female that they were ready for commitment. I would not fail that challenge.

I sniffed the air, expecting my mate's scent to fill my nostrils. Instead, all I smelled was the ancient musk of the forest. Maybe I was too far away still...

I broke into a run. The berries flew from my fingers as I stormed towards the cave. I knew it before I'd even ducked through the entrance. Pria was gone.

Something shattered within me. I howled in anguish, a sound so primal that I surprised myself. I swiped at the roots around me, as if it was their fault she'd disappeared. My nails ached as they sharpened into claws.

Where was my mate?

I forced myself to calm down, pushing the rage and fear down as much as I could. I had to focus if I wanted to find her again. She needed me.

The ground in the cave was undisturbed. If she'd been taken from here, she'd not put up a fight. Maybe she'd been sleeping. Or had she left the tree voluntarily? A cold fist gripped my hearts. Had she left me?

No, surely not. She had to feel the bond between us. And even if she didn't, she had to be intelligent enough to know that I was her best bet of surviving Kalumbu. She wouldn't last on her own. Not because she was weak, but because this planet was designed to kill.

Nobody survived on their own, not even the fiercest warriors.

I rushed outside to inspect the area around the tree. A tiny piece of cloth stuck to a thorny bush. Part of the smart bandage. Pria had been outside, but had she been taken?

Breathing in deep, I searched for evidence of other scents. Nothing. If a predator had passed through here, it had managed to disguise itself well. But there, a footstep in the mud. And beyond it, a mound that hadn't been there before.

As a hacker, I was trained to take in the smallest detail and memorise it in case it turned out to be important in the future.

This leaf-covered hill hadn't been there earlier. It was about as tall as me and twice as wide in all directions; unnaturally symmetric. I raised my spear and pointed it at the hill. It didn't move, didn't give off any kind of scent, but its mere presence was sinister. The purple leaves on top of it were a little too bright compared to the half-rotten foliage on the ground. It was camouflage. But what kind of beast could do this? What could mask its scent so completely? As much as I strained to hear any trace of breathing or movement, the song of the birds high above was the only sound.

Keeping as much distance between the fake hill and myself, I prodded it with the tip of my spear. As much as I wanted to throw it at it from afar, I couldn't risk it. Pria might be somewhere inside it.

As soon as the metal blade touched one of the purple leaves, it shuddered. Definitely not a normal leaf. Around it, other leaves began to shake until the movement ran down the slopes like waves. I jumped back just in time. Where the shaking leaves touched other foliage, it started to smoke. A ring of smoke tendrils now surrounded the mound, making it hard to see what was happening. Krat that. I didn't care how many tricks this thing possessed. I'd force it to give me back my mate.

I stabbed it with the spear again, harder this time. A sharp hiss tore at my eardrums, making me cringe with pain.

"Stop playing," I challenged, ignoring the smoke that filled my mouth. "Show yourself!"

And it did.

Krat.

The mound rose faster than I could process, turning into a column of purple leaves five times as tall as before. And at the top of it, a huge red eye. I'd never seen a beast like it before and I didn't care to ever encounter another again.

In its midsection, a strange bulge broke the otherwise tubular shape. Was that...? Something moved beneath the leaves.

"Pria?" I shouted at the top of my lungs.

Another movement, but I wasn't sure if it was in response to my cry.

"Let her go!"

The monster focused its blood-red eye on me. The black pupil seemed to melt away, revealing a gaping hole.

Without warning, the creature shot forward. I threw myself to the side, evading its maw, but the side of its head crashed into me with a force so strong that I was sent flying back, my spear clattering away. I rolled onto my stomach, coughing and spitting dirt. It wasn't just the impact – the air around us was filled with ashes that tasted of smoke and burnt leaves.

My vision swam. I blinked a few times until the monster came into focus again. It had retreated to its original position, its eye watching me warily.

I fumbled for the spear until my fingers clasped around the metal shaft. Without taking my eyes off it, I stumbled to my feet. This was an entirely different monster than the quecklra. I needed a new strategy.

It had swallowed my mate. When it had opened its maw, I hadn't seen any teeth. Did it swallow its victims whole, waiting for them to be dissolved in its stomach acid? I shivered at the thought that Pria was in there right now.

Maybe I should let it swallow me. I had a weapon, unlike Pria. If I could somehow slice it open from the inside...

The monster didn't let me think. With a hiss, it attacked once more.

This time, I braced for impact. Gritting my teeth, I rolled back and swung the spear at its lower section with all my strength. The blade hit home, ripping through the leaves. I felt resistance and pushed harder, until a loud crunch echoed through the forest.

The monster hissed, this time in pain. It recoiled, its body swaying from side to side and the earth shook with the force of it.

I attacked again and again, aiming for the spot below the bulge. Purple blood oozed from the wound, sticky as tree sap, and the creature started to slow. As I hit the same spot for the fifth time, the leafy skin gave way, exposing a hole that was rapidly growing larger. From above it, something dark pushed against the opening, a sort of leathery sack.

And then, a muffled voice, so very familiar. Pria. She was in there.

I stabbed the creature just beneath the hole. With an anguished hiss, it twisted to the side, unintentionally enlarging the hole. The sack slipped through, and I opened my arms just in time. It was too slimy to grasp, but at least I'd slowed its fall. Inside the sack had to be my mate. It was certainly big enough to hide her, but I couldn't help her just yet. The monster hissed in fury and pain, but it hadn't given up yet. Blood poured from the huge wound, making leaves smoke wherever it hit the ground. Sweat and dirt covered my palms, making the grip on my spear unsteady. I had to finish this quickly so that I could free Pria.

"Let's end this!" I shouted and aimed my spear at the bloodshot eye. The monster quivered, but didn't attack. It was waiting for me to make the first move. Maybe this was a trap, but I had enough. I threw the spear with as much force as I could muster. It flew through the air, perfectly aimed, but just before it hit the eye, the pupil turned into a dark maw again and swallowed the spear.

Krat! I had to hope that the tip had at least grazed its throat, but the beast didn't give any indication that it had been injured further. How was it even still alive with that gaping hole in its body? Surely blood loss alone should have weakened it by now.

It hissed again, so loud that my ears rang. Its eye focused on the sack at my feet as if it only now noticed that it had lost its stomach, or whatever that thing containing Pria was. Hopefully something essential for survival. I wanted the monster to suffer like it had made my mate suffer.

Without my spear, I had no weapons, but that didn't mean I was defenceless. I focused on my hands, forcing my claws to extend further. I grit my teeth at the pain. Not all satyrs had control over this ancient evolutionary trait, but in this moment I thanked my ancestors for bestowing me with this gift. When my claws were as long as small daggers, the pain ceased and I could once more focus on the monster. It was still staring at the sack. Did this thing understand what had happened?

Not that it mattered. While it was distracted, I launched myself at it, embedding my claws at the edges of its wound. I pulled the edges apart with all my might, ripping into the monster's body. Slimy innards pushed against me and I clawed at them, causing as much damage as I could. A dreadful hiss high above me signalled that I had been successful.

The leaves around me suddenly grew slack. I jumped back as fast as I could, but not fast enough to avoid the body of the monster as it crashed to the ground.

10 PRIA

was so thirsty. I blinked up at the dark sky, hoping that it would start to rain so I could drink. Not a single star shone in the night. It was completely dark around me. Was this even the sky?

"You're awake."

Silus. He sounded relieved.

"What happened?"

A cool hand settled on my forehead.

"Do you want the short or the long version?"

I cleared my parched throat. "Both."

"You were swallowed by a monster," Silus said wryly.

Was he joking?

"Can't you remember?" he asked.

I searched my memory, but came up blank. "I was sitting outside waiting for you... that's the last thing I remember."

"You should have stayed inside," Silus growled. "You almost died. If I hadn't come back when I did..."

His voice trailed off. I wanted to argue, say that I had every right to leave the cave when I wanted to, but he was right. I should have known better. This wasn't a normal forest. We were on an alien planet. With monsters that wanted to eat us. And had tried to do so. I shuddered.

"What kind of monster was it?" I croaked. "And do you have some water?"

"I found a stream, I can carry you to it, but we should wait until morning. I don't want to risk walking through the forest at night if we don't absolutely have to. I managed to get as much of the beast's digestive juices off you, but I-"

"Digestive juices?" I repeated. "What. The. Fuck?"

"You were in its stomach," he explained gently. "I cut you out of it... anyway, you don't want to know the gory details. For now, I have some berries that might help with the thirst. I analysed them with my commband and they appear to be safe to eat for Peritans. I've had a few and haven't had any adverse effects."

Yet. The unspoken word echoed between us.

"Alright, I'll try the berries." My voice was so hoarse that it barely sounded like me.

He moved his hand away from my forehead before touching my fingers a moment later. He must have been aware that I wasn't able to see in the darkness. I held my hands together to make a bowl. The berries were cool and smooth, bigger than I had expected, the size of peaches. I took a small bite out of one and sighed in relief when cold juice filled my mouth. It faintly tasted of vanilla, but it wasn't a strong enough flavour to be memorable. The liquid inside was heavenly though. After devouring three berries in record speed, my thirst was gone.

"Better?" Silus asked.

I licked my lips. "So much better. I feel human again. How long did I sleep?"

"It will be morning soon."

That explained why I wasn't tired in the slightest. On the contrary, I suddenly felt filled with energy. My feet no longer hurt, my head was clear, my thirst replaced by a different sort of hunger deep within. I needed *something*, but I wasn't quite sure what.

"The other shelter turned out to be no good," Silus broke the silence. "There are a few more that the AI suggested, but I don't have much hope that they turn out to be better than this cave. At least I know where to find berries and water now, that will keep us going for a bit until we find other resources."

"Are we going to stay here then? For how long?"

"I don't know. If there was any chance of a rescue, we should stay here, not too far away from the crash site. But it's unlikely that they'll come for us. I can scout the area some more and if I find a more suitable shelter, we can move there. Then we'll see."

Wait and see. I didn't like that at all. I wanted action, something to do, a solution to our problem. There had to be a way off this planet. If not, what was the point of trying to survive only to be eaten by monsters at some point? We'd only been here for two days and had almost been killed twice already. That was not a good start.

Silus put a hand on my shoulder. The warmth of his touch stoked the hunger inside me, a desire that had nothing to do with food. I didn't want him to move his hand away again. I wanted him to touch more of me. Feel his hands all over my body.

I breathed in deep, trying to clear my head. This was so unlike me. Maybe the time in the monster's stomach had messed with my head. I dimly remembered dreaming about red eyes, but the memory was all fuzzy.

"I will find a way for us to survive," Silus promised, his voice deep and strangely husky. Was I imagining the need in his voice? Was I hearing what I wanted to hear?

He gently squeezed my shoulder. A croaked moan came from my throat before I could stop myself. Silus froze. So did I. Until I felt his other hand hovering close to my cheek. I couldn't help myself. I grasped his hand and pressed it against my cheek, leaning into the touch. Heat flooded my body, gathering in my core. I felt the first traces of wetness between my thighs. Without panties to soak it up, it was going to be obvious very soon. Maybe he could even smell my arousal already? He'd proven that he had better senses than me. How mortifying... Or at least that's what I should have felt. Instead, I moved my head slightly until my lips grazed his palm.

I kissed him ever so lightly, waiting for his reaction. Silus didn't pull back. I took that as permission to kiss him again, and again, soaking up his warmth. The overwhelming urge to taste him filled my mind. I could have resisted it, but why would I?

When I licked his calloused palm, he cleared his throat.

"Pria..." Him saying my name almost made me faint with need. "There is something I need to tell you."

But I didn't want to listen. I didn't want to stop. I didn't want to hear him say that this was a bad idea, totally inappropriate. All I wanted was more of him. More of his taste, his touch, his warmth. I squeezed my thighs together hard as a wave of desire washed over me. I felt empty. I wanted him inside me. Needed him, so much.

"Pria," he said again, followed by a groan when I sucked one of his fingers into my mouth. I swirled my tongue around it, wishing it was something much bigger, much harder.

I didn't recognise myself. Not that I cared. All I wanted was to feed that hunger inside.

"Touch me," I whispered seductively. "Kiss me."

He hesitated. It was almost enough to break the spell, but then another wave of need pushed away all hesitation. In the darkness, I searched for him until my hands landed on his face. I explored him with my fingers, finding his goatee, his bushy eyebrows, his soft pointed ears, before settling on his horns. They were warmer than his skin, hot almost. Not what I'd expected at all.

"Don't..." he groaned. "Not the horns."

This time, I listened. I cupped his cheeks instead and leaned forward, halting just a breath's width apart from him. I needed to kiss him, wanted nothing more, but I also heard that tiny little voice screaming in my mind that this wasn't me. It was so confusing.

"Are you sure about this?" he asked hoarsely. His breath was hot against my lips. My heart fluttered a little while my core clenched hard.

"Yes. No. I don't know." I huffed in frustration. "Why aren't you kissing me?"

"I think the berries might have intoxicated you. Your pupils are more dilated than they were before. Your heart rate is erratic. You-"

"You can hear my heartbeat?" I interrupted.

"Of course," he said as if that was totally normal. Tsk. Aliens. "I don't want to take advantage of you."

Silus moved back ever so slightly, but I increased my hold on him, trying to stop him from leaving. I still hadn't kissed him. I had to. It would sate that murderous hunger that was once again clouding my mind.

"You're not. I want this. Berries or not. Kiss me."

He sighed. "You're not making this easy, little Peritan."

"Stop resisting," I moaned. "Please."

My thumb brushed over his lower lip. His breath hitched, then he sighed again, louder this time.

"Klat."

He sucked my thumb into his mouth just like I had done earlier. I relaxed my hold on his cheeks, which was exactly what he must have been waiting for. He broke the space between us and I pulled back my hand as fast as I could, just in time for his lips to crush against mine.

It was all I had hoped for and more. He took charge, kissing me passionately, while one of his hands supported my neck, the other caressing my shaved head. His taste filled my mouth, quenching my thirst. I clung to him, the only thing that was safe and real in the darkness. As we explored each other's bodies, our hands roaming freely while our lips were glued together, my thoughts ceased to exist. My past vanished, my fears for the future dissipated, until all that was left was the two of us, right now, right here.

I tightened my hold on him, wrapping my legs around his waist. I never wanted this moment to end.

11 SILUS

She tasted like the sacred honey from the stories, the liquid of the gods. I could have drowned in her. She clung to me, gripping me tightly as if she was worried I'd disappear. I understood exactly how she felt. We'd found each other in the most unlikely of places, surrounded by danger, yet here we were, kissing like there was no tomorrow. It felt better than I could have imagined. Her touch, her scent, her taste, it all made me crazy for more. Yet at the same time, I wasn't sure if this really was her. Had the berries intoxicated her somehow? Or was this simply the relief of surviving the encounter with that monster?

As much as I craved her, I couldn't take advantage of her current state of mind. I would have to be the one to slow the pace, give her time to think, until I could be sure that she wanted this as much as I did. So when her hand slipped beneath my loincloth and wrapped around my hard cock, I gently stopped our kiss.

"No," I whispered hoarsely. "Not yet."

She moaned with need. "I want you."

And I want you. But not like this.

"If you feel the same way in the morning, I will claim you the way you deserve it," I promised. My voice was so husky that I wasn't sure if she'd understood what I'd said. She looked at me with her big, beautiful eyes, tiny stars in the dark night.

Her hand was still on my cock. Klat me, this felt so good. If she kept going like this, I wouldn't be able to hold back for much longer.

"I need..." A moan slipped from her swollen lips. "I need to..."

I understood. "Lie on your back."

She cocked her head, considered my words, then slowly let go of my cock. I suppressed a groan. I'd have to take care of that later, imagining that it was her sacred channel rather than my hand bringing me to fulfilment.

Pria lay back onto the mossy ground, her naked body ripe for me to enjoy. She was so beautiful. I'd tried not to see her that way during the day, pretending that she wasn't fully naked, but now in the sinful dark of night, I couldn't help but stare. Her breasts were firm mounds that begged to be worshipped. Her legs were still loosely wrapped around my waist, her thighs open for me to see her glistening wetness. She looked different there from satyr females, but I couldn't wait to explore just how she would react to my touch. I didn't doubt for a click that we were compatible. We were mates, after all, destined by the gods and the universe to be together. While a satyr female would have had fur on her legs and hips, Pria only had some short black hairs that curled deliciously.

My mate began to touch her breasts, twirling her dark nipples between her fingers. Her back arched a little as she brought herself the pleasure she was craving. I couldn't sit by idly any more.

I scurried back a little, then spread her thighs further. Her scent filled the air, driving me crazy with need. Not wasting another click, I plunged between her legs, my tongue finding her wet centre.

Pria gasped at the sudden sensation, her body tensing up.

She let out a moan, her hips gyrating in pleasure. I moved my tongue up and down her slit, my lips sucking strongly on her slick nub. As she began to writhe with pleasure, I moved faster and harder. She called out words that I didn't understand yet that reverberated in my heart. My tongue flickered over every inch of her most sensitive parts, sending waves of arousal through her body. Her breathing became ragged as I continued to thrust my tongue deep inside of her, exploring and tasting every part of her until she was panting hard.

I slowed down a little, wanting to prolong the pleasure. I licked at her in long slow strokes, exploring every inch of her with my tongue. Her hips bucked up as I hit a particularly sensitive spot and I held on tight as she writhed in anticipation.

I tasted her sweet saltiness and felt her muscles ripple as I explored further. She was so incredibly responsive.

I kept pushing deeper inside of her, teasing out all the secrets of her pleasure spots until she finally came undone beneath me, screaming her release. The feel of it against my tongue sent shivers up my spine and I could feel myself explode against my loincloth.

But it wasn't over yet, not for her. I slipped a finger inside of her, stroking delicately while maintaining a steady pressure with my tongue. The combined sensations made Pria cry out in ecstasy, driving me wild with need to be closer to her. I made her come a second time, relishing in her taste, only stopping to lick her when she'd finished quivering beneath me.

Finally, when her pleasure had subsided, I withdrew my finger and crawled up beside her. I took her in my arms and held her close, breathing in the sweet scent of her bare skin. I kissed her softly on the forehead before she snuggled up against me, contented and sated. Her eyes were closed and her breathing slowed. I watched as she slipped into a peaceful sleep, smiling and feeling like I'd never been happier.

I was still keeping watch over her when she woke with a soft yawn.

"Good morning, mate," I said with a wide smile, before realising my mistake. Had she noticed?

Her smooth forehead turned into wrinkles as she slowly opened her eyes to look at me. "Mate?"

Klat. I should have kept my mouth shut.

"Mate?" she repeated when I didn't respond. She sat up and wiped the sleep from her eyes. I wanted to tuck a strand of her silky mane behind her ear but resisted the temptation. I had to fess up first.

"I have to tell you something," I began while trying to figure out just how to broach the subject. "I was going to wait until we've found a way off Kalumbu, but now... Klat."

She crossed her arms in front of her chest. Was she hiding her nakedness from me or was she simply showing that she was upset?

"How much do you know about satyrs?"

Pria grimaced. "Absolutely nothing apart from what you've told me. Which isn't much at all."

"Yes. Sorry. I know. So..."

"Just say it," she snapped. She was wide awake now, her amber eyes blazing with impatience.

"Satyr society has very strict traditions and-"

"Why did you call me mate?" Pria interrupted. "I don't want a lesson in satyr culture. Not now, anyway. Tell me what's going on."

I groaned internally. How was I going to fix this? "You're my mate," I blurted. "My star-given, gods-sent mate."

I waited a bit to let the news sink in. Was she going to be overjoyed? No, it didn't look that way at all. When I looked at her, I saw a storm darkening the horizon. The first thunder was about to crash down on me.

"What does that mean?" she asked in a strangely monotonous voice.

"Satyrs mate for life. They might experiment a bit, but usually we wait until we find our true mate. Or mates, in rare cases. We always know when we meet your mate. It's like they have a sign painted above their head. It couldn't be more obvious. So when I saw you on the screen, I knew-"

"Screen?" Pria's voice had turned icy. "Saw me? You watched me?"

Even though she didn't move, I felt a distance settle between us.

"I will start from the beginning. Please, promise you will listen until I'm done?"

Her glares hurt, but she nodded. "I promise, but I want the full story. No gaps, no secrets, no lies. Understood?"

For a moment, I admired my feisty mate, then sobered again. This was going to be hard. I was not good at talking. I could write flawless code, but words were difficult. They could have so many meanings and were so easily misunderstood. I wished I could write her a programme that would answer all her questions in my stead.

"Alright. I told you about the Artep, the ship I live on. A while ago, we stopped at the Kalumbu space station for supplies and to refuel. It's not a pleasant place, but it's the only station in this part of the galaxy. While we were docked there, two aliens approached Captain Twim and asked for passage on the Artep. Qong, a Gofren, and Penny, a Peritan, the same as you. Twim made a deal with them to let them stay on the Artep in exchange for labour. Penny has some engineering skills, so the plan was for her to keep our ship running. The Artep isn't new and has lots of issues... Anyway. The two of them ended up watching the Trials of Kalumbu and spotted another Peritan female in the footage. I don't know what Penny and Qong promised the captain to get his support, but he decided that we would help rescue the female from Kalumbu. By then, Fay - that's the other Peritan - had already been fighting for her life on this planet and had met her mate, an orc named Vruhag. I hacked into the game makers' system, and we managed to get them onboard the Artep."

I could see Pria was getting impatient, but she needed to know the full story.

"During the hack, I pulled a lot of data. I'd planned to sell it for profit, but that's when I found something odd. There was a record of other Peritans-"

"Humans."

"Yes. I am told that's what you call yourselves. Sorry. So, I discovered that other Peri...humans were kept somewhere on the Kalumbu space station. Twim ordered us to watch the Trials coverage to find them. And that's when I saw you. I knew immediately that you..."

"Yes?"

"That you were mine." I watched her for her reaction. She didn't give anything away, simply stared at me with her beautiful brown eyes that were the colour of my fur. Yet more proof that we were meant for each other.

"How did you know that?" she asked eventually.

"I felt it in my hearts, in my horns, in my entire body. I looked at you and suddenly I felt complete. Like a hole in me had been filled. I knew I had to find you. I went to Captain Twim and told him we had to launch a rescue mission. He refused. So I stole a shuttle and came down here myself. They shot some missiles at me and during my evasive manoeuvres, I crashed. You know the rest."

Pria frowned at me. I could sense her confusion. It was a lot to take in. The Peritans on the Artep had explained that their species didn't believe in mating for life. They didn't have the same intrinsic urge to find their one true mate. I'd have to be patient with her.

She ran a hand along her shaved head. I was so tempted to caress the stubble, kiss her forehead. I balled my hands into fists to stop myself. She needed space to think, that much I understood.

Finally, she spoke. "What if you're wrong?"

12 PRIA

was trying to get my mind around it all, but I was failing. Aliens. Mates. Hearts.

"Wait, did you say hearts? Plural? You have more than one?"

He put a hand on his bare chest. I tried to ignore just how sculpted, perfect, hard his physique was.

"Yes. Two hearts. One here. The other here."

Alright. Two hearts. Totally normal. Don't freak out. It would be a strange reason to finally lose it. I'd been okay with being swallowed by a giant worm, but now I was having trouble? Get it together, Pria. Two hearts were no problem at all. Everything else was.

"What if you're wrong?" I repeated. "How can you be sure?"

"I know it," he said simply. "There is no doubt in my mind or in my hearts. You are my mate. We are destined to be together."

I wanted to jump up and run. He sounded way too possessive. This wasn't romantic. It was scary.

"What if I don't want to be with you?" I challenged.

His ears drooped, reminding me of a sad puppy. "I don't know. I wish I could say that I would accept it, but I don't know if I can. It is getting harder to hold back."

Alright, now he was scaring me.

"Hold back from what?"

His ears went up a little, as if he was getting hopeful. I had to make sure he wasn't getting the wrong idea. I was only gathering more information, not encouraging him in his delusions.

"Claiming you," he rasped. His voice was so husky. Like last night. Oh no. What had I done? What had I let him do to me? I dimly remembered begging him to fuck me. He'd refused. Made me come apart with just his tongue and his fingers. I couldn't help but look at his hand, still pressed against his naked chest. Those fingers had been inside me. My core throbbed with the memory and desire. No, I wasn't going down that road again. It had been a one-off. I'd lost control. Maybe it had been the berries, maybe the relief at surviving my encounter with the worm. I was glad that he hadn't gone all the way. He could have easily taken advantage of me. I would have welcomed it last night, but now I was grateful that he hadn't.

"I'm not sure what to say," I admitted. "Am I supposed to feel the same way? Is that why I... why... last night..."

I couldn't say it. My face was burning with embarrassment. I didn't know what I was feeling anymore. What was real and what was due to this situation? He was a gorgeous, attractive guy, despite the horns and the hooves and the tail that was currently curled around his thigh. And he'd come to rescue me. I was grateful for that, of course, even though we were now both stuck here. Was there more? I didn't want to delve deeper. It was too crazy to even consider that my attraction was caused by something other than my own mind and my silly hormones.

"I will give you all the time you need," Silus promised. "I now wish I'd asked the Pe... human females more about how they realised that they had alien mates. I know that both of them are sure that they found their mates, but I don't know how they came to that conclusion. Maybe they felt it. Maybe they believed in the stars. Maybe... I really don't know. I'm sorry."

"Maybe we can ask them once we get off this planet," I said, sounding way more optimistic than I felt. "For now, I'd appreciate it if you didn't turn into a dick-driven macho and instead focus on how we can survive this. Deal?"

He grimaced. "Deal. Let's start with getting you some water. I found a stream yesterday, but I have nothing to transport water with, so I shall carry you there."

I was about to protest that I could walk, but then remembered that my legs were still covered in bandages. It was a miracle that they'd survived the encounter with the worm's stomach. Alien technology was kind of cool.

My stomach growled, reminding me that water alone wasn't enough. "Did you find any other food? I'd rather not eat more of those berries if I can avoid it."

Silus chuckled. "I did not, but maybe we will be lucky. There is little luck to be found on Kalumbu and I feel like I have already received my fill by encountering you."

My cheeks only grew hotter. He said such sweet things even though he didn't seem to be aware of how romantic he really was. If we'd been back home and he'd been human, I may have been interested in taking this further. Go on a few dates, find out more about him, meet his family. Slow and steady until I could be sure that he was right for me. I'd wasted most of my twenties hooking up with guys only to realise I kept choosing the wrong men. I never learned from my mistakes until I slowed down and didn't follow my impulses.

"I will quickly check that it's safe outside. Stay here."

I rolled my eyes at him, but I'd learned my lesson. I wasn't going to tempt fate again by wandering about the forest by myself. I waited patiently, ignoring my rumbling stomach, until Silus returned a few minutes later.

"I could smell the scent of a predator nearby, but it was an old trace. We should be safe. I will carry you."

He hooked his arm under my knees and wrapped the other around my back, then lifted me easily. I tried to ignore that I was naked. By now I should be used to it, but it still sucked not to have clothes. Not like he wore much more than me. His loincloth didn't leave a lot to the imagination.

"Maybe we can find some big leaves that I can make into a dress?" I suggested while he carried me out of the tree cave. "Not that I have any sewing skills, but I'd love to have something to wear."

"I will find you something," he promised. "Are you cold?"

I shook my head, bumping my cheek against his hard chest. "No. But I feel vulnerable without clothes. Do you ever wear more than just a loincloth?"

For some reason, he chuckled. "No. I only wear this when I'm surrounded by aliens. Back home, we all walk around naked. Clothes are only used to cater to the sensibilities of visitors."

A planet full of naked satyrs. I tried not to imagine what he was hiding under that loincloth. Just how alien was he? Did he even have a penis or was I thinking too much like a human? Maybe he used his tail... I pushed that thought away while squeezing my thighs together to stave off the heat gathering in my core. Not the time to think of that.

"The stream is just beyond there," Silus said, oblivious to my internal struggles. "My commband analysed the water and deemed it safe for our consumption, but it said the same about the berries and we know how that turned out."

"Right now, I'd drink anything. And I'm almost ready to eat a piece of that worm. Scratch that. No, I'm not hungry enough for that."

Silus laughed, his chest rumbling against my cheek. I loved that sound. He needed to laugh more often. Not that we had a lot to be cheerful about on Kalumbu.

We continued walking in silence - well, Silus walked, I let myself be carried in his arms - and I found my mind drifting back to what he'd told me earlier. He'd said he'd watched me from his ship. That meant someone had been filming me. A horrible thought made a cold shiver run down my back.

"Are they watching us?" I asked. "Do they know where we are?"

"It's very likely. I spotted a camera drone shortly after I crashed, so I bet they filmed our battle with the quecklra. Unless they have really small drones, they haven't been inside our tree cave, but I'm not sure how advanced their surveillance tech is. If we're really, really lucky, they will think that you were eaten by that monster yesterday. I'm not an official contestant, so they might not be tracking me. It's hard to know. I will let you know if I spot another drone."

"Thanks," I muttered. "I hate the thought of them watching us. It's so invasive."

"I know. I wish I could protect you from them. Undo all the damage they did. I'm sorry we didn't meet under better circumstances."

So am I. But I didn't say it out loud. I couldn't. I didn't want to get his hopes up. There was nothing between us other than the drive to survive. Once we were safe, we'd go our separate ways. I'd go back home to Earth, somehow, and resume my old life.

Could I do that? After all that I'd seen and experienced? Back in my cell, I'd thought about what my family would think. They knew me well enough to know that I hadn't just run away. I called my mum every day during the week, so for me not to let them know where I was should have rung alarm bells. They'd probably searched for me. They would have involved the police. Maybe the media.

My old life wouldn't continue just like it had. I would have to answer questions, explain what had happened. And of course, nobody would believe that I'd been on an alien planet fighting monsters. I laughed to myself at the thought of telling my mother that I'd been swallowed by an alien worm. She'd call her friend Iris, a clinical psychologist.

No, I had to stop deluding myself that I could just go back to normal, even if I somehow made it off Kalumbu. I was a different person now.

Somehow, that made me feel a little lighter. I had options. I wasn't bound to returning to life as I'd known it. Maybe I could let my family know that I was okay and then spend some more time exploring space. I'd only seen Kalumbu, the most hostile of places, but there had to be other worlds that were less deadly.

13 SILUS

I took a slightly longer route to the stream so I could carry her in my arms for a little longer. It was selfish and dangerous, but I couldn't help the urge to keep her pressed against my chest where she was safe.

The forest around us looked deceptively calm today. Birds and smaller animals were moving around in the canopy, their song and scents wafting down in the light breeze. Occasionally, I saw some larger tracks on the muddy ground, but they were a few days old. I didn't tell Pria about them. I didn't want to frighten her unnecessarily. She'd already encountered some of the worst Kalumbu had to offer. If we were lucky, any predator we came across from now on would be less dangerous. I knew I was deluding myself. This was the calm before the storm. We weren't safe. But we both needed this moment of peace to recover from all that had happened.

When we finally got to the little stream, I didn't let go of Pria. I focused my senses, extending them as far as I could, searching for any threat that may be lingering in the undergrowth. An old scent hung to the fallen tree to our right, where a predator must have rubbed itself against the bark. Again, it was at least two days ago. We'd be fine. I should lower my mate to the ground, let her drink from the stream. But something stopped me. An instinct that not all was as peaceful as it seemed. It was either a predator that could shield its scent, or something else, something even more sinister.

I scanned the air above us for the sparkles that often gave away camera drones. Nothing.

"What's wrong?" Pria whispered.

"I don't know. Something feels off."

She didn't argue with me. I was glad she trusted me enough and didn't insist on being let go of.

I didn't know what to do. Was I just imagining things? Was my urge to protect my mate influencing my rational thought? I'd heard of males going insane with need if they couldn't claim their mate. But this wasn't that, right? It was too early. I wasn't crazy. I wasn't imagining the sense of impending doom that was gripping my hearts.

"Should we go back to the cave?" Pria muttered. I should tell her at some point that the translator implant would work even if she only mouthed the words without the use of her vocal cords.

"I don't want you to be thirsty. We will be fast. I'll set you down, you drink as much as you can while I stand watch, then we will return to our shelter as fast as possible."

I didn't think it was a good idea, but I couldn't let her die of thirst. She needed to stay hydrated, or she'd wither away.

"Alright. I'll be as fast as I can. Is this water definitely drinkable? It looks very muddy."

"My commband says it is and it didn't do me any harm, but there is no guarantee. I'm sorry."

"It's not your fault. I'll just have to risk it."

I took one last cautious look around us, then gently lowered her to the forest floor until she was sitting at the edge of the stream. I straightened immediately, every muscle tense, my senses on full alert. I was going to defend my mate with my life. I heard her take large gulps of water, but I didn't dare to look down in case I missed a threat. That ominous feeling that something was about to happen was still getting stronger. I really hoped I was wrong. We deserved to have a break. We deserved to live.

"Look," Pria suddenly hissed. "There are bubbles in the water. What are they?"

I stared at where she pointed. Columns of small bubbles rose from the muddy bottom of the stream. Those hadn't been here yesterday, or at least I couldn't remember seeing them. The stream wasn't deep enough to hide a large predator, unless...

I reached for my mate at the same time as the stream exploded into a flurry of water and mud. Huge jaws snapped at her outstretched arm, missing her by a hair's width. Tentacles erupted from the boiling surface, blindly reaching for us. I managed to get a hold of Pria even while she slipped into the water, pulling her back, wrapping her into my arms, and then I was running, not looking back, running and running until we reached the tree cave.

I didn't let go of her even when we were safely inside. I was breathing hard, not just because I'd run faster than I ever had in my life, but because the terror of almost losing her was clawing at my mind. It had been so close. She'd almost been taken from me.

I clung to her, squeezing her against my body, vowing to never let her get so close to harm again.

"It's okay," she whispered gently. "We're safe now."

She stroked my heaving chest with her soft hands. It only made me want to grip her tighter. She was so precious, so soft, so vulnerable, so wonderful. She was mine. My mate.

"We're not safe." I could barely speak. "We will never be safe while we're on Kalumbu. We have to get away from here."

She smiled at me wryly. How could she smile after almost being taken from me?

"That isn't news. It's not like we have a way to get off the planet, though, do we? You said your ship is unlikely to help us. And even if they wanted to, how would they know where we are?"

"The beacon!" I exclaimed. I wanted to smash my head against the cave's wall for forgetting all about it. Since taking the smart bandages from the survival kit, I'd completely ignored our small but vital supplies. I finally lowered my mate to the ground, making sure her injured legs were stretched out, then rummaged through the kit bag. The water purification tablets were useless without a container for the water, but I handed one of the nutrient bars to Pria.

"Let's not risk eating berries again. This doesn't taste like much, but it will sustain you for a while."

I didn't take a bar for myself. I would stick to whatever I could forage and save them for my female.

We had a few more smart bandages left, although I hoped we wouldn't need them. The only other item in the survival bag was the beacon.

"How does it work?" Pria asked in between munching on her nutrient bar.

"It will send a distress signal that will be received by anyone listening on the intergalactic emergency frequency. All ships usually automatically scan that frequency, although not all do it for benevolent reasons. Space pirates see ships in distress as easy pickings, but I doubt any of them would risk breaking through the security surrounding Kalumbu. No, our main worry is that the game makers will pick it up and come for us. Or worse, send some of their worst monsters or contestants our way. If they lost track of us with their camera drones, this will be a sure way for them to find us again. But it could also reach the Artep. Captain Twim may have reconsidered by now, or the Peritans may have persuaded him to help us... It's hard to know. Turning on the beacon is a huge risk."

"Not turning it on isn't much safer, is it? It's not like we're going to survive like this for much longer. No, don't lie to me. You don't have to pretend. I know our chances of making it out alive are tiny. I've understood that by now. I still don't get how they chose me, or how I even got here, but it doesn't really matter. I vote we turn on the beacon."

Without thinking, I pulled her against me and kissed her forehead. She stiffened for a moment, then chuckled and wrapped her arms around me. My cock hardened at the sensation of her soft hands against my back. Klat. This was not what I should be thinking about just now. I had to focus on our survival.

"If you want to turn it on, then we shall do that," I whispered. She smelled like the forest around us, but underneath was her own sweet scent that drove me crazy. I should let go of her now. I should be sensible and rational. Why was it so hard? I was a grown male, not a young buck who didn't have control over his dick. I brushed my lips over the smooth skin just beneath her hairline. Heavenly. She didn't stop me, so I moved lower, kissing her eyebrows, the ridge of her nose, her warm cheeks.

"What are you doing?" she laughed. "That tickles."

"Does it?" I slowly licked her skin. "Does this?"

"Yes...no... shouldn't we be turning on the beacon?"

I sighed and kissed her one more time, committing the sensation to memory.

"You are right, of course. I got carried away."

I leaned back and checked that my loincloth was covering my erection. Barely. I looked at Pria and realised that she'd followed my gaze and was now staring at my crotch. Her lips were parted slightly; I didn't think she was aware of just how enticing that made her look. This female was going to drive me crazy if I wasn't careful.

"Beacon," I grunted and pulled the small silver disk from the survival bag. "Now?"

14 PRIA

Silus no longer seemed capable of forming full sentences. Neither was I, for that matter. He hadn't even kissed me on the lips just then, yet it had felt a hundred times more special than any normal lips-on-lips-kiss I'd had in the past, with human men. I'd wanted more, still wanted more. So did he, if his tented loincloth was anything to go by. I really wanted to know what he was hiding underneath. Hopefully, this wasn't the day we made a terrible mistake and died. I fully intended to survive.

"Yes, let's do it," I said, surprised at how hoarse my voice was. Maybe it was the lack of water. Oh, who was I kidding, it was not because of thirst. That kind of thirst. I was thirsting for Silus in ways that I didn't recognise. I'd never felt this need for someone in all my life. It was strange and alien and scary. Not as scary as staying on this planet, however. Priorities.

He handed me the disk. It was about the size of my palm and had a single round indentation at the top.

"Press your finger there and hold until pink lights flash."

"Pink?"

"Yes, pink for emergency."

I suppressed a laugh. I did not associate that colour with emergencies, unless you counted fashion emergencies.

I held my thumb against the indentation. A soft vibration went through the disk, but it took another ten seconds before it turned bright pink and vibrated again.

"What now?" I asked.

"Now we wait. The beacon transmits our precise location, but it will take some time for anyone to get here, friend or foe. Maybe you should rest."

I didn't feel tired in the least. Adrenaline was coursing through me.

"It's a pity we no longer have the spears. Should we make other weapons?"

Silus pulled a small knife from the belt holding his loincloth in place. "I have this, not that it will do us much good. If the game makers decide to end us, we won't stand a chance."

"Still, I would feel better if I had something to fight. Even a stick would do."

I looked around the dark tree cave for a loose root.

Silus got to his feet. "If it will make you feel better, I will get you a stick. And then I will sharpen it for you."

He ducked out of the cave, knife poised. I watched until he was out of sight, then munched on the last bite of the nutrient bar. As the satyr had promised, it was fairly tasteless, a bit like a stale oatcake, but it had certainly vanquished my hunger. I was a little thirsty, since I'd never got to drink much at the stream, but it couldn't be helped.

I'd only had a glimpse of the monster that had risen from the muddy bottom of the stream, but it had looked like a cross between a crocodile and a kraken. Without Silus, I'd be dead. To be fair, I wouldn't have even made it to this day. He'd saved my life several times already. That had to be the reason why I felt safe with him. Even though we were in the most dangerous place I'd ever been, I felt this strange calm whenever he was near. Like I could go to sleep without fear of nightmares. Like he'd be able to fend off anything and everything. Like he had only my best interests at heart.

It was ridiculous. I didn't want to feel any of this right now. This was hell in space. I should be focusing on surviving, not on a hot alien. I was an independent woman who'd got through life on her own, mostly anyway, a few fast-ending relationships aside. I didn't need a guy, especially not one that wasn't even human. I should keep my distance from him.

"I got you a stick," Silus announced from outside. "And a fruit that my commband says is edible."

He entered the cave, a proud grin on his face. He looked adorable. It instantly made me forget all about my resolutions. I really needed my hormones to go back into hibernation and let my brain take control.

He dropped a bundle of branches on the ground, then presented me with an aubergine. I stared at it, unable to believe my eyes. Maybe this was a dream after all. It looked exactly like an aubergine back on Earth: purple, smooth, oval, slightly phallic. I tried not to laugh. I really did. But I failed.

I snort-laughed, looked at the aubergine again, then started giggling hysterically. All the tension of the past few days flowed from me, turning into high-pitched giggles.

"What's wrong?" Silus asked with real concern in his deep voice. "Is it affecting you? Are you having a reaction to it? The commband said it was safe, but..."

"It's... not..."

I gasped for air in between bursts of laughter. This wasn't real. Couldn't be.

"Do you need something? Medicine? Water? Tell me."

He sounded frantic but seeing him stare at the aubergine in fear made me erupt into new fits of giggles. It was just too much to take.

"...you...emoji..."

Silus stared at me, his ears lowered, his brow furrowed. "I don't understand."

He kneeled at my side and gently patted my back. Tears ran down my face as I tried to get my breath back, but then he sat the aubergine down in front of his loincloth and it began all over again.

Fuck. My. Life.

When I finally calmed down enough to breathe and wipe my cheeks, I didn't find words to explain what had been so funny. In retrospect, it wasn't quite as hilarious as it had seemed only minutes ago.

"Are you better now?" Silus asked cautiously, looking at me as if I was a delicate flower about to wilt in his hand.

"Yes. Sorry. Not sure what came over me."

"Everyone reacts differently to being in the Trials. I have seen contestants rage, laugh, cry, and every other emotion you can think of. Sometimes those moments were harder to watch than people being torn apart by monsters. When someone who went into the Trials full of strength and ambition ends up just a broken shell of themselves, it's heartsbreaking."

"Ah yes, two hearts. I almost forgot about that."

"Two hearts for twice the love." He cringed as if he regretted saying that. Was there a romantic hidden in his horned, hulking alien?

For a split second, I debated asking whether he had two of other things, but stopped myself. Instead, I grabbed one of the sticks he'd brought. "Can I borrow your knife?"

"Let me cut open this fruit first. This might be our last meal on Kalumbu."

If we were lucky. Or terribly unlucky and were about to die.

I didn't look at him as he worked on the aubergine. I didn't need another giggling fit as a hundred eggplant emojis flittered through my mind. I had to focus on what was important. Like the stick in my hands that might have to become a weapon. I broke off a few smaller branches, then proceeded to work on the next stick. And still I didn't dare look at Silus and his fruit, even when it started smelling like honeydew melon in our tree cave, sweet and refreshing. Not the worst final meal.

"Ready," Silus announced. He waited for me to put down my sticks before handing me a slice of fruit the colour of beetroot.

"Is this going to make me... horny again?"

"I don't believe so. I adjusted the parameters in my commband to mark the berries as unsuitable for Peritans, I mean, humans, so hopefully this fruit won't have any side effects."

"I'll take you at your word. I don't want to be distracted when they come for us."

I didn't expand on who 'they' might be. Friends or foes. Somehow, I assumed someone would come. I hadn't even considered that nobody would pick up our signal.

We'd be condemned to stay on Kalumbu for how long? Forever? Until we were killed, anyway. I didn't expect us to have a long life. Maybe a quick death by the game makers would be preferable.

"Go on, try it. It's really quite delicious."

While I'd been lost in thought, Silus had managed to get his goatee soaked in fruit juice. It almost looked as if he'd dyed his beard beetroot red. It suited him, in a punky way. He'd already devoured three slices of alien-aubergine and didn't seem to be suffering from any adverse effects. I looked down at my slice. Maybe being horny in the face of danger wasn't the worst thing that could happen.

I took a bite. A firework of flavours exploded in my mouth. I felt my eyes widen and my nostrils flare. It shouldn't be possible to taste this *much* at once. Sweet, salty, sour, umami, all mixed together, all intense and overwhelming. I couldn't identify any flavours I recognised, it was too much, too delicious, and I needed more. I finished my slice in record time before accepting my next one from Silus.

He grinned at me, clearly amused at how I'd scoffed down the fruit. I ignored him and got to work on the second portion. I tried slowing down to make it last, but it was just too good.

"Where did you find this?" I asked in between bites. I didn't care that I was talking with my mouth full. Manners weren't really important in the face of almost-certain death.

"Just outside behind a bush. The wind must have blown away the leaves that were covering the plant, or we would have seen it earlier. There were a few more fruits growing from it, so I can harvest them later. Maybe slow down a little. It can't be good to eat this fast."

"You ate three slices in less than a minute."

"I am a satyr," he said simply, as if that would explain everything. Maybe it did, to him.

It took some persuading to have him give me a third portion of what I now called the fruit of paradise. If this was to be our last meal, at least it had been one worthy of celebrating our lives.

Suddenly, Silus jumped to his feet and grabbed one of the sticks. "Someone's coming."

15 SILUS

'd assumed we'd have to wait longer for the signal to be picked up, but if someone had been listening on that frequency, it wasn't impossible for the Artep to have come for us. If they somehow managed to get through Kalumbu's defences without my hacking skills. Some of the other members of Twim's crew knew how to get around basic security, but it had been a struggle even for me to hack into their barrier last time. Unless they had help from the same mysterious person who'd assisted me, it was unlikely that they were here already.

If only I'd used the time to sharpen some spears instead of indulging in having a meal with my mate. The sticks were little better than nothing. They'd break as soon as they hit the hide of any beast, but at least they might distract it for long enough to help Pria to flee. I'd fight tooth and claw to give her a chance of survival, no matter how small. She could survive without me. I couldn't without her.

With my knife in one hand and a stick in the other, I ducked out of our cave. I'd heard the sound of a shuttle or vehicle nearby, which could only mean that someone had come for us. We'd not seen or heard any machines in our time on Kalumbu.

I should have said goodbye to Pria, I thought while scanning the area around the tree cave. I should have kissed her.

A familiar scent hit me. I breathed in deep just to make sure. Of all the people I expected, he wasn't one of them.

I waited outside the cave, protectively hiding the entrance with my body just in case I was wrong and this wasn't who I thought it was. The sound of someone moving through the trees had me grip my stick tighter. It was a reflex, not because I was about to attack him.

"What's happening?" Pria whispered from inside the cave.

I stayed quiet, unwilling to raise her hopes. I could be wrong. This could all be another trick the game makers were playing on us. I wouldn't put it past them. They loved to toy with contestants, giving them hope only to pull it away at an instant. It broke people. I wasn't going to let them break my mate. Nor me. We'd get out of this, somehow.

When he came into view, I couldn't help but stare at him in disbelief. Was he real?

"Fancy seeing you here," Vruhag smirked, raising one fist in greeting. "Where's your mate?"

The orc was dressed in battle gear, a huge axe in one hand, several blades and guns strapped around his waist. Just like me, he preferred to keep his chest bare, something his mate, Fay, seemed to appreciate.

"I didn't think you'd ever want to set foot on Kalumbu again," I told him. "Of all the people on the Artep to come, you would have been the last I'd expected."

Vruhag chuckled. "Trust me, it wasn't an easy decision, but I'm the only one other than Fay who's actually been on the surface. I know this planet. I know how the game makers think. So, it made sense for me to come. But we're wasting time. The shuttle is parked in a clearing since you didn't pick a good spot to land for your shelter."

"Who is he?" Pria asked from behind me, popping her head out of the cave. I resisted the urge to reprimand her for not staying where she was safe.

"This is Vruhag, the orc I told you about."

"You've told her about me? Did you tell her of my strength, my prowess in battle, my-"

"Turn around," I snapped at him. "My mate is naked."

With a cheeky grin, he turned his back. "I might be able to help with that. I didn't know what condition you were in, so I brought a medical kit. There's an emergency blanket inside."

He detached a small pouch from his belt and pulled a golden ball from it. At the shake of his fist, it unrolled itself into a blanket large enough to cover even me. If only my survival pack would have included one of those. Pria would have been a lot more comfortable.

I snatched the blanket from the orc and handed it to Pria. "Wrap yourself in it, then I will carry you to the shuttle."

"Is she injured?" Vruhag asked sharply.

"Yes, but nothing the med pod won't fix."

"Cursed Trials. I can't wait until we free the other humans."

I again realised hadn't told her the worst thing about her abduction yet. It hadn't made sense to upset her while we were fighting for our lives on Kalumbu. Once we were safe, I'd tell her. Somehow. I wasn't looking forward to it.

"I'm ready."

I ducked back into our cave where Pria was sitting with the blanket wrapped around her like a towel. Her shoulders and arms were still bare, which made sense considering the temperatures outside.

I pulled her against my chest and carried her outside. Vruhag had still turned his back to us dutifully, but I was sure that if he sensed the smallest threat, he wouldn't be this relaxed.

"Lead the way," I commanded. "Let's get off this cursed planet."

"With pleasure."

The shuttle was parked not far from the cave, but with every step, the fear that we might not reach it increased. I tightened my hold on my mate. It would be just like the game makers to throw something at us just when we thought ourselves safe.

When it came into view, I quickened my steps. Vruhag did the same, his posture tense. He probably felt the same way. I would have to thank him properly for returning to this place of horrors. I'd watched him during his own Trials, seen what he'd been through. He'd been gravely injured just before we'd rescued him and his mate, although he'd been unconscious for that rescue. Once on the Artep, he'd been in the grip of some sort of mating fever that affected orcs who didn't claim their mates. It had been scary to witness.

Now that we were closer to the shuttle, I realised that it was not one I'd ever seen on the Artep.

The shuttle's ramp slid down at the same time as the doors opened. Vruhag ran up the ramp and disappeared inside to start up the engines. With Pria in my arms, I was slightly slower.

I heard the arrow before I felt it bite into my shoulder. My right arm went slack. Pria would have slipped from my grasp if her arms hadn't been wrapped around my neck.

"Silus!" she shouted and for a terrible moment, I thought that she may have been hit as well. But no, she was staring at the forest behind us, at whoever had shot me.

Her shout had alerted Vruhag. He came running out of the cockpit, took one look at the situation, before pushing a button on the wall that would pull up the ramp. With a metallic groan, the doors behind me slid shut. We were safe.

"I can take her," Vruhag offered, holding out his arms towards my mate.

"No," I snapped. Seeing my mate touched by another male would hurt more than the injury.

Pria gently put her hand on my cheek. "I can stand by myself. Don't worry about me. Let me down and then we'll look at your wound."

I didn't want to let go of her. Her touch distracted me from the raging pain in my shoulder. Whatever had hit me had dug deep. If I was unable to move my arm, it must have severed important structures.

"Is there a med pod on this shuttle?" I asked the orc.

"Only a very basic one. It won't heal you, but it will administer potent painkillers that can help until we get back to the Bloodstar."

"The Bloodstar? Not the Artep?"

"No. A lot has happened since you left. I will explain later. Now set down the female and let me take you to the med pod."

Reluctantly, I let Pria slide to the floor. She stood, but didn't look very steady.

"Help my mate to a chair first," I ordered. "She can't stand for long."

Pria rolled her eyes at me. "I'm not the one bleeding all over the floor. Stop being a hero and let him help you."

I looked down at the puddle of blood around my feet. That would explain why I felt light-headed. Maybe going to the med pod wasn't such a bad idea after all. With one last look at my mate to make sure she was alright, I followed Vruhag to a side room only large enough to harbour a few crates and an old-fashioned med pod that had seen better days. Better decades, actually.

"And this thing still works?"

Vruhag growled at me and lifted the lid. "Get in before you pass out. I don't fancy hauling you in there by myself."

I flashed my teeth at him, but my vision was starting to get foggy. This wasn't the time to fight the orc. I sat at the edge of the pod, then lowered myself into it. Before the lid even closed above me, everything descended into darkness.

16 PRIA

My stomach lurched as the shuttle took off. I'd found a seat belt and had fastened it around my waist just in case. The big green orc had disappeared to fly the ship and Silus was in the med pod, which left me all by myself. My feet hurt a little, probably a sign that the bandages needed changing, but I wasn't going to mention it until I could be sure that Silus was feeling better.

What had even happened? One moment I'd been sure that we were finally safe, the next his hold on me had loosened. I hadn't even realised that he'd been hit until I'd seen the blood dripping down his back. It had looked bad, but hopefully the med pod, whatever that even was, could fix him.

The room had no windows to look out of, so I didn't know what was happening outside. Were we still near the surface or at a safe distance already?

"Silus?" I called cautiously. What was the other alien's name again? Of course, my brain chose this moment to forget. He'd looked fearsome with his green skin, his tusks and bulging muscles. He was about as tall as Silus, but bulkier. For a moment, I distracted myself by imagining who of the two aliens would win in a fight. The orc was big, but Silus had horns and claws. I'd seen the satyr fight. He'd moved surprisingly gracefully for his size; a warrior who'd turned his body into a weapon.

A screen appeared on the wall opposite, startling me. The green alien smiled at me from the screen, or at least I assumed it was supposed to be a smile. His tusks got in the way of making him look friendly.

"Silus will be in the med pod until we get to my ship. Give me a moment, then I'll help you to the cockpit."

The screen changed to a view of the forest below us. We were already further up than a plane would fly, but the planet was still too close for my taste. I'd only feel safe once it was a speck of dust in the night sky.

From this far away, the colours of the trees blurred into a muted palette of purples and blues. A huge river cut through the jungle like an ancient scar, dividing it in half. A few clouds drifted beneath us, but they barely hid the planet from view. How many contestants were still down there? How many of them were fighting for their life at this very moment?

I hoped Silus was going to be alright. It was only one wound. The scars on his body told of many previous injuries. Hopefully, this would be just another scar for his collection.

The shuttle lurched to the right without warning. I gripped the sides of my seat, wishing there were armrests to hold on to. Hopefully, Silus was safe in the med pod. He had to be strapped in, right?

"Sorry for the turbulence," the orc announced through speakers. "We should be fine from now on. I can't leave the cockpit just yet, but I'll be there shortly."

I didn't want to sit here on my own for one more minute. If I couldn't be with Silus, I'd at least get to ask the other alien some questions about what was going on. Silus clearly hadn't expected the orc to be the one to rescue us. He'd also been confused about the name of the ship. Now that Silus wasn't able to make plans for us, it fell to me to find out about the situation we were in.

I undid my seatbelt and carefully stood up. My feet hurt more than they had in quite some time, but I only had to imagine the pain Silus was in to be able to push it aside. Once we were on the proper spaceship, I could hopefully get some painkillers. Until then, I just had to hold it together.

I hobbled to the door, hoping that the shuttle wasn't about to lurch again. The door slid open, revealing another one straight ahead and two to either side.

"Straight ahead. I should have known you're as stubborn as the other Peritans."

I grimaced at the orc's comment and approached the door in front of me. It didn't open immediately, only when I pushed my palm against it. A long yet narrow room awaited me, chairs similar to the one I'd sat in on both sides. In the centre were floating tables that moved out of my way when I limped towards them. Handy. Furniture that moved. When I reached the other end of the room, I took a look back. It was kind of satisfying to see that the tables had returned to their original position as if nothing had ever happened.

Behind the next sliding door was the cockpit, not unlike that on a large airplane, with two pilot seats and lots of screens, switches and buttons. The orc sat in one of the chairs, making it look like it was made for a child.

I couldn't help but groan in relief when I took a seat and could stretch my legs. The orc didn't take his eyes off the screen in front of him but rummaged in a hatch to his left. He held out whatever he found in there for me to take.

"What is that?" I asked, staring at the grey strip of what looked like cardboard.

"Painkiller. Chew it."

I didn't question him whether it was safe for humans. His mate was a human woman, so he had to know.

The strip felt as dry as it looked when I took it into my mouth, but as soon as I started chewing it, it turned into lemon-flavoured jelly. Was I supposed to chew the jelly or swallow it? The orc wasn't looking at me, so I discreetly swallowed about half of it and kept the other half in my mouth just in case.

"How is Silus?"

The green alien tapped a button and a screen in front of me changed to offer a view of a metal cocoon. It had a small glass window at the top through which I could just about make out the satyr's face.

"You can watch him. He's asleep. Won't wake until we get to the Bloodstar."

"Is that your ship?"

"Yes."

"Is your woman...mate there?"

"Yes."

Well, this orc wasn't very chatty. Maybe it was because he had to concentrate on our flight, but I had so many questions that needed answering.

"Will they come after us?"

"Maybe."

"How did you get through the barriers? Silus said he hacked the game makers' system; did you do the same?"

"No."

If I'd been his mate, I may have slapped him. Luckily, I wasn't. Silus wasn't the best at communication either, but at least he could produce sentences that were longer than a single word. I resisted the temptation to ask the orc if he'd ever been told that his verbal skills were lacking.

"If they come after us, do we stand a chance?"

He sighed. You and me, both.

"Maybe. Probably not."

Great. So we weren't safe yet. I should have felt scared, but I was strangely relaxed. Cheerful, even. Was there something in the painkillers that had influenced my mood? If so, that orc better be oblivious to the side effects of the medicine he'd given me. If he'd intentionally drugged me, I'd have some choice words for him. Or better, I'd let Silus do the talking. I bet my satyr wouldn't be happy about someone sedating me.

"How long until we get to your ship?"

"Not long."

"Are you intentionally being taciturn?"

To my surprise, he chuckled. "My mate doesn't like it if I talk to other females."

"Wow, a full sentence!"

Oh, had I said that out loud?

The orc threw his head back and roared with laughter.

"I like Peritans. You are funny."

"So you are an orc?"

"Yes. Vruhag is my name, in case Silus forgot to mention that. And my mate is Fay, a Peritan like you."

"He mentioned you both."

Vruhag grinned. "I'm glad he did. He and his crew pulled us from that blasted planet. Although it turns out Twim's generosity only went so far..." His grin disappeared. "I'll tell you the full story later when Silus is awake. We're getting closer to the Bloodstar. Just a moment, I'll make your screen mirror the outside view."

The metal cocoon with my sleeping Silus - wait, not *my*. The Silus. A Silus. Certainly not mine. I felt my cheeks heat up and hoped Vruhag wasn't looking my way. I stared at the screen in front of me instead which now showed the dark of space. We must have broken through the atmosphere and were now in orbit of Kalumbu.

Something glinted on the left edge of the screen, quickly growing bigger.

"That's the Bloodstar," Vruhag announced proudly. "My ship."

It was not how I'd imagined a spaceship. It kind of looked like three spheres squashed together until they resembled a part of the Very Hungry Caterpillar. Around them was a silver halo, reminding me of the rings of Saturn. I couldn't see whether it was solid or small pieces moving so fast that they turned into a blur. Was that what was powering the ship? I thought about asking the orc, but I doubted I'd understand his answer. I knew nothing about mechanics, physics, or even how exactly my little car worked. As long as it drove when I put my foot on the pedal, I was happy. It was going to be the same with this spaceship.

"It's pretty," I said when I realised Vruhag was waiting for my reaction.

He grunted something inaudible. I clearly hadn't responded in the way he'd hoped.

"I've never seen a spaceship before," I explained apologetically. "Are they all as shiny as yours?"

"No, they're not. The Bloodstar is special. I won her from a rich gazillionaire when he bet that I couldn't beat his pet lacooda in a fist fight." Vruhag pointed to a scar on his right bicep. "It wasn't an easy fight, but worth the pain. I've never had a ship like the Bloodstar, and I never will again."

Wow, so many words in one go. Was this the normal Vruhag, or was he just particularly excited to get back to his ship and his mate?

A pink light flashed at the edge of my vision, followed by a string of curses from the orc. Most of them didn't seem translatable, but I did understand the final bit.

"...they klatting found us."

17 SILUS

I smelled my mate before I even opened my eyes. It made the pain a little more bearable.

I'd been drifting in and out of consciousness for what felt like a small eternity. Every time I'd tried to cling to reality, I'd been pulled back into darkness. The pain had spread from my shoulder down my back and thighs until my entire body seemed to be engulfed in flames. There must have been poison in the arrow.

Now that I was finally able to stay awake, the pain had dulled somewhat, but I was sure that the med pod hadn't fixed me. Yet I'd rather be conscious with my mate by my side than sedated and pain-free.

The lid of the med pod lifted with an angry hiss. How ancient was this pod? It hadn't done much to lessen my pain. Hopefully Vruhag had better tech on his ship.

"Silus? Can you hear me?"

Her voice was the sweetest thing I'd ever heard.

"Mmmhpwhr."

My voice didn't work as intended. A straw was pushed against my lips almost immediately and I greedily drank the offered liquid.

"Yes," I croaked after I'd drank my fill.

"I need you to get up and transfer yourself onto the stretcher," Vruhag commanded.

My vision was fuzzy. All I could see was blurry shapes around me. I recognised my mate by her scent, mixed with the sharp twang of Vruhag's odour. Had he always smelled this vile or was this because he was too close to my female?

"I can't see," I admitted. "Where are we?"

"We've docked onto the Bloodstar," the orc said impatiently. "But we need to get off this shuttle as fast as possible. We've got incoming. So get your arse out of that pod. I'll help as much as I can, but you're too heavy for me to carry."

My mate took my hands and gently guided them until I felt a soft mattress. "There's a stretcher here that you can lie on. It floats."

She sounded in awe. This all had to be very overwhelming for her. I wished I could be the support she needed right now, but instead, I was an invalid with a barely functioning body and impaired vision. What else was that poison doing to me? I'd seen the effects of some of the plants found on Kalumbu. The ones that weren't deadly were so painful and horrific that the victims cried for death. This one was either slow or the med pod had diminished the effect somewhat.

With Vruhag's help, I managed to heave myself onto the stretcher. I tried not to cry out in pain when my shoulder hit the mattress. Pria pressed her cool hand against my forehead. It felt so good, not just because my skin seemed on fire.

"You can't walk," I remembered. "You should be on the stretcher, not me."

I sat up, but Vruhag pushed me back. Before I could complain, he'd wrapped a safety belt around my chest and my legs. Kratting orc.

"The stretcher should be strong enough to carry you both. May I lift you onto your mate?"

"He's... yes."

What had Pria been about to say? Did she want to contest that she was my mate? I hoped not. I thought she'd accepted it by now. Surely, she had to feel it. Peritans were different, but they had to have some sort of sense that made them recognise their mates.

I balled my hands into fists when I heard the orc put his hands on my mate's hips. Luckily for him, he let go of her as soon as she was safely lying on top of me. I wrapped her into my arms, breathing in her scent.

"Am I hurting you?" she asked, her voice full of worry. "I can sit between your legs if this hurts your shoulder."

"No. It's fine."

It did hurt, but I wasn't going to let her know that. I forced a smile. "Let's go."

The stretcher's movement was barely perceptible. I was glad it was a smooth ride. That way I could focus on how my mate was pressed against me, her back on my chest, the stubble on her scalp gently tickling my skin. My cock was hard despite the pain, pushing against her legs. Was she aware of it? Did she know how much I desired her even in this state? I would have claimed her right now if she'd asked me to, pain be damned.

My balls ached. I shouldn't be thinking of how it would feel to slide between her thighs. I imagined it would be like coming home, a home I'd only ever dreamed of in the sleepless hours of the night when I felt the loneliness of space pressing down on me.

"Almost there," Vruhag announced, followed by the hiss of opening doors. That had to be the airlock between the shuttle and the ship. "Fay is waiting to bring you to the med bay while I deal with our pursuers. Try to get into the pods as fast as you can. It might get very bumpy once they catch up with us."

A moment later, a familiar scent reached me, pleasant but not tempting to me in the slightest. Fay was a pretty female, but I had my own.

"Hi, I'm Fay," she introduced herself to Pria. "Vruhag! You took your time." The wet smacking of lips made me jealous.

"Sorry, mate. I came back as fast as I could."

"I know, I'm just teasing. Now go deal with our new friends while I take these two to the med bay."

"They aren't our friends... ah, it's one of those Peritan phrases."

On top of me, Pria chuckled. She clearly saw some parallels between this couple and us. I smiled. Hopefully, we'd be as close as Vruhag and Fay soon.

The stretcher began to move again. The sound of doors opening and the rhythmic patter of Fay's footsteps were the only way I could orient myself in this unfamiliar ship.

"Where is Captain Twim?" I asked weakly.

Fay laughed coldly. "I don't know and I don't care. When he refused to help the two of you, we decided to go our own way. Luckily, they located Vruhag's ship around the same time you stole the shuttle, so we were able to leave the Artep and come for you ourselves. I think some of your old colleagues were tempted to abandon Twim, but in the end only Qong and Penny came with us. They're on the bridge just now."

I was too weak to swear, but I mentally cursed Twim.

"Can you believe that he wanted us to pay him for his expenses?" Fay continued. "He shut up when Penny reminded him how she'd already saved him tons of money by fixing several systems on the Artep."

A cool woosh of air made me shiver.

"That's us in the med bay. I'll park the stretcher next to the minor injuries pod for you first, then Silus gets to heave himself into the major injuries one."

I realised she was talking to my mate. "Pria," I croaked. "Her name is Pria."

As much as I didn't want to let go of her, I also needed her wounds to be healed. Knowing that she was still in pain was worse than the agony in my shoulder and back. She tried to hide it, but I was her mate. I was created to care for her wellbeing. I'd always know if she was hurt.

When Pria climbed off me with Fay's help, I felt bereft. If only there were med pods big enough for two people at once. Technically, the two of us could have squeezed into one because Pria was so much smaller, but the pod's AI would be confused by that. It might even think that we were one organism split in half and attempt to merge us. No, I didn't want to merge with my mate in *that* way.

I heard her pod close with a low hiss.

"I'll turn on some music for you, Pria," Fay said cheerfully. "It can get a bit boring in these pods. But it won't hurt, don't worry. Now on to you, Silus. Your pod is to your right, can you sit up and wiggle your bum over? If not, I can activate some of the medical bots to help. Penny showed me how they work."

"No, I will manage."

I was not going to be assisted by bots. I was a satyr in his prime, not an invalid.

The pain was indescribable, but I somehow made it into the pod. As soon as I lay down, the foam-like material grew all around me, cushioning me while also holding me in place.

"It says it has to sedate you for the treatment," Fay announced. "Sweet dreams!"

I closed my eyes and hoped that it was going to be over soon.

18 PRIA

as this how a newborn felt? My skin seemed softer than it ever had before. My hair had not only regrown by three inches, but was also silky and smooth, my teeth cleaner than after a visit to the dentist, and even my fingernails felt sturdier. The med pod clearly hadn't just healed my feet and legs, but also removed any impurities and signs of ageing. As soon as I found a mirror, I'd check if the tiny wrinkles around my eyes had disappeared as well.

Fay had provided me with a simple dress, slippers and some underwear that had come fresh from the processor, whatever that meant. She'd promised she'd have more clothes created for me once we were at a safe distance from Kalumbu. The ship had jerked from side to side a few times, but that was all I'd noticed. Sitting here in the med bay, a circular room with five metal cocoons - much shinier than the one on the shuttle - I felt completely out of the loop. But it had been my decision to stay with

Silus rather than accompany Fay. The other woman had promised she'd return soon, once she found out what was going on.

The screen on Silus' pod said that his healing was about halfway done. At least I assumed that's what the progress bar meant. While I could understand both Silus and Vruhag when they talked, the translator the aliens had fitted me with clearly didn't work on the written word. Whatever language the screen showed looked like strange squiggles to me.

I rubbed the back of my ear where Silus had indicated that the translator implant sat. I couldn't even feel a scar there. It was yet another violation against my body that the game makers had done. Compared to the torture and experiments, it may have seemed small, but I didn't know how it worked. Did it change my brain somehow? Was it permanent or could I have it removed when I returned to Earth?

The progress bar slowly grew a little more. This pod didn't have a window through which I could watch Silus, so there was nothing to do but stare at the screen. Maybe I should have gone with Fay after all.

I stretched my legs, marvelling at how there wasn't even a scratch to be seen. It seemed like magic. Doctors back home would give anything for this technology. What else could these pods do? Cure cancer? Regrow limbs? It was a shame I couldn't just pack one of these pods into my suitcase - not that I had one - and take it home.

Home. I missed my family. I missed my flat, my job, my friends. How long had I been gone for? I'd been imprisoned by the aliens for what had felt like at least a month before I'd been transported to Kalumbu. A few days there with Silus and I likely wouldn't return home right away. So let's say two months. How long had it taken for my abductors to take me here?

My memory of that day was fuzzy. I remembered teaching an afternoon yoga lesson at the local community centre. After that, my mind was blank. Had I made it home? Had someone snatched me on my walk back? Or had I been taken from my bed at night? In the beginning, I'd racked my brain, trying to remember, but it had been in vain. Now, I didn't even try anymore. It didn't matter. I was here, far away from Earth. I had to focus on how to get back, not on how I'd come to be here. I couldn't exactly go to the game makers and demand to be returned home. They'd put me right back into the Trials.

Why were Penny and Fay still here? Had they decided to stay with their mates rather than return to their old lives? Or was there a different reason?

Something cold and clammy wrapped itself around my heart. What if we were too far away to return to Earth? Or maybe nobody knew where Earth even was. They called us by a different name, Peritans rather than humans, but what if we weren't actually Peritans and they were confusing us with a different species?

My head hurt. I had to stop worrying. First, I'd wait until Silus was healed. He would have answers for me.

And even if he didn't, I knew that he would help me in any way he could.

I touched the pod, stroking the smooth metal as if it was the satyr. I missed him. It was ridiculous; he was right here, right in front of me, with only the cocoon separating us, but I still couldn't get over the need to touch him. I wanted to be back in his arms.

Get it together, Pria. I wasn't going to be able to stay with him. He couldn't come to Earth with me, not with horns, hooves and a tail.

Behind me, the door slid open without so much as a warning. Fay walked in with another woman whose blonde curls were barely tamed by the red scarf she'd wrapped around her head. That had to be Penny.

Before I'd even taken a step towards them, Penny wrapped me into a hug.

"It's so good to finally meet you! Of course, we've been watching you in the Trials, but it's so much nicer to meet in person."

Fay chuckled darkly. "Isn't it just. Kalumbu isn't exactly a place for picnics and afternoon tea."

"Speaking of picnics, we brought you some food. You must be hungry."

Penny finally let go of me and presented me with a round box about the size of a dinner plate. "We thought you'd want to stay here, but if you don't like this, we can also go into the canteen and you can choose something from the food fabricator."

Curiously, I removed the lid. A heavenly smell of fresh waffles hit my nose. I blinked, suddenly feeling strangely emotional. I'd expected strange alien food, not something that reminded me of home. Inside the box were three round pancakes with a rough honeycomb pattern etched into the surface.

"Pancakes? Or waffles?" My voice broke and I made sure not to look at the two women. I didn't want them to see just how close to crying I was.

"My version of waffles," Penny laughed. "I've been trying to programme the fabricator to make them in the right shape, but this is as good as it gets without a proper waffle iron. I've not given up yet, though, so you might get real waffles eventually. I've become pretty handy with alien technology."

I remembered Silus telling me that Penny had worked on the space station above Kalumbu for years before her rescue. I couldn't wait to hear her full story.

I rolled up one of the pancake-waffles to make it easier to eat and took a bite.

"Oh my, that is so good!"

Penny gave Fay a triumphant grin. "Told you she'd want comfort food."

Fay giggled. "Wait until you meet Penny's mate. You'll know then why she loves waffles so much."

The blonde woman rolled her eyes. "It's a total coincidence."

"What is?" I asked while eating. I hadn't even realised how hungry I was, but now I was sure that three pancake-waffles weren't going to be enough.

"Qong has a very strong resemblance to a waffle," Fay laughed. "And according to Penny, he even smells that way to her."

"That's private!" But Penny was also grinning widely. "You'll get to meet him soon. Right now, the guys are busy on the bridge, but it looked like they were about to shake off our pursuers. The Bloodstar is way more advanced than Kalumbu's ships, so it shouldn't be long until we get the all-clear."

"And what happens then?" I asked, now on my second pancake-waffle.

The two women exchanged a look. Fay ran a hand through her auburn hair. "How much did Silus tell you?"

"He said that after rescuing you, they discovered that there were other humans held on the space station. It's why he watched the Trials and saw me in them. Have you found any other women since or was I the only one?"

"There is at least one other," Fay said with a deep sigh. "But Silus is the best hacker and when he left to find you, the search kind of stalled. We got a glimpse of one woman in the Trials coverage earlier today, but the stream changed almost immediately, and we've been unable to find any footage of her again. If both of us hadn't been watching it together, we would have probably thought it had been a mistake. Now that Silus is back, he might be able to find a trace of her in their systems."

I looked at the med pod's screen. Three quarters done.

"Does it always take this long?" I asked.

"It totally depends on the patient's injuries," Fay explained. "Vruhag was in one for ages when we got rescued. I remember how it felt, helpless to do anything but watch. But Silus isn't as badly injured as my mate was. He'll be fine, you'll see."

Penny peeked at the screen, apparently able to read the squiggly language. "Yes, it's already in the final stages. His injury has been healed completely, now the system is just working on purging every trace of the poison from his body."

"Poison?"

"Yes, whatever struck him must have been poisoned. Who attacked you?"

"I don't know. It happened so fast. We were almost on the shuttle when he got hit. Maybe it was another contestant?"

"Likely," Fay nodded. "One of the game makers' drones would have created a much worse injury. Or killed him instantly. He was lucky. Both of you were."

"I don't feel lucky," I admitted.

"I get that," Penny nodded. "It's hard to see the positive. But you'll get there. Trust me. I've had a lot of time to think about it all."

"How long were you at the space station?"

"At least two years, but I'm not entirely sure. I didn't exactly keep track of time in the first few weeks."

Her expression darkened and I quickly changed the topic before she was overwhelmed by memories. All three of us had our traumas. This was not the time to compare notes.

"Can I have some more waffles?"

19 SILUS

Once again, my mate was with me when I awoke.

"Treatment complete," a soft mechanical voice announced. The lid of the med pod opened, giving me a full view of my beautiful Pria. Something had changed. Her scalp was no longer covered in brown stubble; she now had a mane that reached to the tips of her ears.

My vision was as clear as ever. All pain was gone. The pod had done its job.

I sat up and rolled my shoulders. There was no trace of lingering injury.

"It's good to see you," Pria breathed. She smiled at me, but there was something sad about her expression.

"What's wrong?"

"Nothing. I'm glad you're awake again."

"I'm your mate. I sense that you're not happy. What's wrong?" I demanded, now on full alert. Had one of the males on board this ship threatened her? I was going to kill them.

I jumped out of the med pod, pleased to see that I still wore my usual loincloth. Some med pods melted away all clothes, and since my belongings were still on the Artep - unless Twim had destroyed them - I didn't have any other clothes. As much as I wanted Pria to see me in all my naked glory, I doubted Vruhag and Qong would like me parading my manhood in front of their mates.

"Nothing is wrong. It's just all a bit much. I've been talking to Penny and Fay and..."

Oh no. Had they told her? No, Pria wouldn't be this calm if she knew. I had to tell her soon before she found out from one of the others.

I opened my arms and to my relief she stepped into my embrace. I hugged her tight, careful not to squeeze her trembling body too much. She was delicate, yet I'd seen how strong she was despite her physical shortcomings. She'd survived Kalumbu. Not many people could say the same.

"It's alright," I whispered, breathing in her sweet scent. "Everything will be alright."

I almost believed it.

"Did we get away from the game makers?" I asked gently.

"Yes. Fay told me a few minutes ago. I asked them to let me be alone with you when you wake up, but they're all waiting for us on the bridge."

I hugged her a little closer. She'd wanted to be alone with me. That meant a lot. On Kalumbu, she'd been forced to be with me, she'd not had any other option, but now that she had two other females of the same species to spend time with, I was happy she chose to be with me instead.

I kissed the nape of her neck, making sure my horns didn't touch her face, while monitoring her reaction. Her heartbeat galloped in response. She wanted it, too. My tail wrapped around her leg before I even knew what it was doing. My horns throbbed with need. I wanted to claim her. Was she ready for it?

"You smell so good," I muttered before kissing her again.

To my surprise, she chuckled. "Do I smell like waffles to you?"

"Ah. You spoke to Penny."

"I did. And she made me waffles, or at least what passes for that in space."

I suppressed a growl. Someone else had provided food for my mate. It should have been me. At least none of the other males had dared to. They were well advised to keep their distance until I'd officially claimed Pria as mine. The thought of them anywhere near her made my muscles tighten with anger.

"What's wrong?" she asked. "You're suddenly all tense."

I forced myself to relax again. "Just the thought of you being in danger. But now we are safe."

She leaned back so she could see my face. She smiled up at me, her eyes lighting up like gemstones.

"Yes, now we're safe. Are you going to kiss me?"

I was barely holding on to my sanity. The urge to claim her right here, right now was threatening to take over. "Do you want me to?"

She licked her lips, almost driving me over the edge. I wanted that tiny pink tongue in my mouth.

"Yes."

There was no holding back. I kissed her hard, wrapping one hand around the back of her neck to steady her as I plunged my tongue past her lips, claiming her mouth. Her hands roamed my naked back and I willed her to move further down, but her nimble fingers grabbed my hips instead, clinging to me as I drowned in our kiss. She tasted like the birth of a new universe. Hope, beauty, love.

The horror of the past few days drained from my mind, leaving nothing but desire for my mate. This was what it felt like to be with her without being surrounded by danger. We could take our time, focus on just each other, ignore everything else. There wouldn't be a monster jumping out of the shadows. There'd be no poison in the food I was going to feed her. Only Pria and me, forever.

She moaned, her fingers digging into my skin. She wanted more. I was going to give it to her.

But not here. Not in the med bay.

Ending the kiss was like surfacing from a beautiful dream. I hated doing it. But I also needed to make this moment special for her. Pria deserved so much better than the floor in this sterile room.

I put my hands on her hips and scooped her up. She wrapped her legs around my waist. The scent of her arousal permeated the air, making my cock harder than ever.

I walked us to a terminal near the door and held my hand against it. Almost immediately, Vruhag appeared on the screen.

"I was wondering when you'd wake up."

"I am awake. And I need a room."

Vruhag snorted with laughter. "We have already prepared one for you. I remember what it was like. I'll send a clean bot to guide you. But don't take too long. We have much to discuss."

"Don't take too long," I muttered as soon as the transmission ended. "You should have seen him and Fay after we rescued them. Didn't resurface from their cabin for days."

Pria sucked in a breath. "Are we really doing this?"

"If by 'this' you mean me claiming you as my mate, then yes, we are."

Her heartbeat accelerated, but it wasn't from fear. Her arousal was obvious. I couldn't wait to get into a private room where I could worship her body like I'd dreamed of ever since I'd laid eyes on Pria.

A small cleaning bot flittered into the med bay, hovering a hand's width above the floor. Three lights on its back blinked, then it turned the way it had come, leading us through the Bloodstar's unfamiliar corridors until it stopped in front of a nondescript door. As soon as I held my hand against the scanner, the door slid open. The bot drove away, having done its job. I bet Vruhag and Qong were sitting in the bridge, watching us, probably laughing. They knew what it felt like, the moment before you finally got to claim your female. They'd both already done it.

This was my moment. Our moment. When we turned from two people from opposite sides of the universe into a star-blessed couple.

"Wow, this is beautiful!" Pria exclaimed when I walked us into the room. "Look, there's even flowers! How did they get flowers in the middle of space?"

A large bed covered in smooth, clean sheets took up half of the cabin. Back home on Faunus, I would have taken her on the fur of a beast I'd killed myself, but this would have to do. Opposite the bed was a table decked with filled glasses, a bowl of snacks and a beaker containing flowers. I wasn't quite sure what their purpose was. Were they edible? Did Peritan females like to nibble on plants before or after the claiming?

"Would you like a flower?" I offered, trying to be patient.

"No, but is that something to drink? I'm rather thirsty after all those sweet waffles."

I sat down on one of the chairs but kept Pria on my lap. I wasn't ready to let go of her just yet. Sniffing the glasses told me it was a light alcoholic beverage that the other females were partial to.

"I believe Penny calls this 'meet'," I explained while handing one glass to Pria. "It is similar to a drink you have on your planet."

"Meet? I don't think I know that one. Oh, wait. Mead! Yes, it smells a bit like honey. This is delicious!"

I'd had some of this drink before and while I enjoyed it, I would have preferred one with more alcohol in it. This barely even made my horns tingle.

Pria leaned against my chest, her hair tickling my skin. I breathed in her scent, simply enjoying the moment.

"We need to talk."

Her words took me by surprise. That didn't sound good. Was she having doubts? Did she not want to proceed with the claiming after all?

"What's wrong?" I asked, trying to keep my voice level. I didn't want her to know just how worried she'd made me.

She shifted her position until she could look at me. I wrapped an arm around her back, supporting her.

"I had a lot of time to think while you were in that med pod," she began slowly. "And I feel like we need to be on the same page. We've only known each other for a few days, but I really like you. If I'm honest, I don't think I've ever liked anyone as much as you. But... how is this going to work? Logistically. I'm human, you're a satyr. We're from different planets. I'm just thinking of the future, how it could even be possible for us to be together? You can't walk around on Earth looking like you do. They'd lock you up, experiment on you. Humans don't know that aliens exist, so you can't come with me. But I miss my family. I want to go back home. I don't think I could stay here forever."

My hearts grew heavy. I'd thought I had more time before I told her the truth. Time for our relationship to grow, so that I could support her better once she found out. But she had to know. I had to tell her.

I emptied my glass in one go, wishing it was a stronger drink. I could have done with some liquid courage.

"I have something to share with you that might help, but it will also hurt. I am sorry that I'm the one to have to tell you."

Her brow furrowed, her eyes widened a little. "I have a bad feeling about this."

"And you'd be right to. I didn't want to mention it while we were on Kalumbu. You needed all your energy and focus to stay alive. But now that we actually have a future, you have to know." I didn't know how to start. How could I lessen the impact of the painful truth?

There was no easy way of telling her. And I was scared. I didn't want to lose her.

"When I hacked into the game makers' system and found information about you and the other Peritans, I discovered something very unexpected. All of you had been brought to the Kalumbu space station at the same time. They transported you in cryo tubes. And..."

"Yes?"

Pria bit her lip, looking nervous. I sighed and wished I didn't have to do this.

"You were in cryosleep for a long time. They preserved you as you were the moment you were abducted, but time passed while you were asleep. A lot of time."

Her lips quivered as she asked that horrible, horrible question.

"How long?"

"In your way of counting, about seventy years."

20 PRIA

pward facing dog. Exhale. Push into downward facing dog. Breathe. Jump into forward bend. Exhale.

I went through the sun salutation again and again, clinging to the familiar rhythm of inhale and exhale. I ignored everything around me, focusing only on the way my muscles stretched and ached, the air in my lungs, the cold floor beneath my feet.

Mountain pose. Start again. Breathe.

I didn't find the equilibrium I sought. My mind wouldn't shut up. No matter how much I tried to get into the flow, let go of all the thoughts getting in the way of inner peace, I just couldn't.

Seventy years.

An entire lifetime.

Arch your back. Feel the breath exiting your lungs as you exhale.

My parents were dead. My aunties and uncles were dead.

Plank, make sure shoulders are over wrists. Exhale.

Most of my friends were dead. Maybe all of them. Everyone I knew. And in a way, I was dead as well.

Breathe. Breathe. Breathe. Don't forget to breathe.

I sank into child pose, making myself small. All the children I'd known, my nephews and nieces, would be grown adults by now. Some may not even be alive anymore.

I pressed my forehead against the cool floor of the spaceship, wishing the cold would freeze my frantic thoughts. I supposed I was grieving everyone at once. My heart wasn't strong enough for this. I couldn't feel this much sadness.

"Pria?"

His voice was low, gentle. He wasn't sure what to do. He'd been watching me, but hadn't intervened when I'd launched myself into my sun salutations, desperate for something familiar in this unfamiliar world.

I didn't know how to reply. I understood why he hadn't told me until now, but I was still angry. Not at Silus. At the world. At the entire universe. Why was I even still alive? What was the point?

I let myself roll onto one side and wrapped my arms around my legs. As much as I wanted to cry, my eyes stayed dry.

"Do you want me to hold you?"

He sounded so helpless. In a way, I wanted to say yes. I didn't want to be alone. But at the same time, he was living proof that I wasn't home, surrounded by my family. Without Silus in the room, I could perhaps pretend that the last half hour had never happened. I could imagine going back to Earth where everyone was waiting for me. Back to my old life.

It hadn't been a particularly exciting life, but I had been happy. Most of the time. I'd done my best. I'd been a good daughter. I'd loved my job. I'd enjoyed spending time with my friends.

Now, I only had Silus. The only person in the entire universe who knew me even slightly.

I had to be one of the loneliest people alive.

"I'm here for you. Whatever you need."

I believed him. I knew he'd do anything to make me feel better. Maybe I wasn't quite as lonely as I thought. I still had him.

"Yes, hold me."

My voice was barely a whisper.

He was there in an instant, wrapping himself around me like a cocoon, protecting me from the world. Our bodies fit together perfectly. There was nothing sexual about our embrace. He was simply holding me, steadying me through his presence, while I finally felt the first tears spring from my eyes.

We lay there until I began shivering from the cold. Silus was warmer than me, but the cold from the ship's metal floor was seeping into my bones.

"Let's get you into bed."

He carefully lifted me off the floor. Again, I was amazed at just how gentle this big man could be. The bed was warm and cosy, especially when he draped a blanket over the two of us. Again, he spooned me from behind, one arm wrapped around my waist. If I listened really closely, I could hear the soft beating of his hearts. Ba-ba-bum-bum. I focused on the steady rhythm as I let myself drift off into sleep, hoping Silus' comforting presence was going to protect me from nightmares.

Fay and Penny took one look at me and knew immediately. They hugged me and we had another cry, all three of us. The only humans in this part of the universe, except for the woman - or women - still hidden away somewhere on the Kalumbu station.

The three guys stood a little apart, giving us space. Both Qong and Vruhag had helped their mates through this, just like Silus was going to help me. We'd never done what we'd set out to when we'd gone to that room, but somehow, I felt closer to him than ever. Surviving Kalumbu had made us friends. Dealing with my grief might turn us into something even stronger.

When Fay disappeared to make us all some food, Penny showed Silus and me around the ship. Well, parts of it. It was huge, like one of those gigantic cruise ships that were basically floating cities. Not that this ship was built to house thousands of people. It only had room for a crew of about a hundred, while the rest of the space was reserved for cargo and weapons systems. According to Vruhag, it had been a trading vessel when he'd acquired it, but he'd since added various modifications to make it suitable for a battle-loving orc.

While it looked like a caterpillar from the outside, the only reminder of the ship's shape were several circular or oval rooms. Most corridors had a sloped ceiling, making it feel like walking through a tunnel. I quickly lost track of my bearings. I'd have to ask if I could get a map. When Penny led us to the swimming pool, I gasped. I hadn't expected this at all. And not just any swimming pool. One with a huge window - or screen that looked like a window - with a view of the stars. I would have loved to have jumped in right away, but I was in dire need of breakfast. Not that I knew what time it was. This could have just as well been dinner. I'd slept for what felt like a long time, and then Silus and I had snuggled some more in bed. Again, he hadn't pushed me. Just gentle hugs, a few tame kisses. I appreciated that he was giving me time. As tempting as mindless sex would be to help me forget the agonising truth, I also wanted our first time to be special.

Penny also showed us a comfy lounge with moving furniture that could be arranged as needed, followed by a virtual reality room that blew my mind yet again. Silus promised me a demonstration later on. There was also a gym with strange contraptions that kind of scared me, a holo cinema, an observation lounge to watch the stars, a bar slash man cave, and finally the dining hall which they called a canteen. It was surprisingly cosy, not as utilitarian as I'd expected.

"There's an actual kitchen next door, but most of the time we use the processors over here," Penny explained. "They can create almost anything as long as you give them the correct recipe."

"Where do they get the ingredients?" I asked, thinking of the waffles from earlier. I doubted they had access to fresh eggs and milk in space.

"Nutrient blocks," Silus butted in. "You don't want to see them in their natural form. They contain all the most common food molecules, and the processor then selects and arranges them in the right manner."

Penny laughed. "He's right, it's best not to think about it too much. You'll get used to it. But Fay has been cooking actual food to celebrate your arrival. Luckily, the Bloodstar's refrigeration chambers kept running even after Vruhag was kidnapped by the game makers, so we have lots of fresh supplies for cooking. As I said, most of the time we don't bother, but it's nice to have the option."

A gong echoed through the room, followed by Fay's cheerful voice. "Food will be served in the canteen imminently. Please take your seats."

"What time is it?" I asked while Silus programmed the furniture to arrange itself into one big round table surrounded by six chairs.

Penny checked a device on her wrist that looked similar to the satyr's. What had he called it, commband?

"Time here isn't calculated in Earth hours, but I'd call this lunch. If you want it more accurately, you'll have to do some maths. We're running on intergalactic time and one IG day has 27 hours. An hour is divided into clicks rather than minutes, with one click about one and a half minutes. Actually it's something like 88 seconds, but... You didn't want all this information, did you?"

I chuckled. "Knowing that this is lunch helps already. My inner clock is totally confused."

"It'll take a while. Fay still hasn't got used to not having sunlight to tell her what time of day it is. I lived on the space station for so long that I've kind of forgotten what the sun even feels like... or fresh air... or wind..."

Even though she was smiling, I could hear the sadness behind her words. I couldn't imagine being in space for two years.

Fay's arrival saved me from having to come up with a reply. Rather than carry a tray full of steaming bowls and plates, it was floating in front of her, apparently following her commands. Wow. It looked like magic, even though I knew it was technology. Behind her, Vruhag and another alien entered the room. Now that I saw the infamous Qong, I understood what Fay had meant about him resembling waffles. He was covered in thick golden scales that looked like perfectly baked waffles. His hair was arranged in a wild mohawk, giving him a somewhat rebellious appearance. Just like Vruhag and Silus, he seemed to be allergic to shirts. At least he wore actual trousers, not just a loincloth. Maybe I could get Silus to put on some clothes eventually. Not because I didn't want to see him naked, but because it distracted me. No guy should look this good without a shirt.

Somehow, Fay directed the plates to move into place in front of each of us while the larger bowls settled in the centre of the table.

"Tuck in," she encouraged us once everyone was seated. "Before it gets cold."

"What is this?" Vruhag asked, his nose twitching.

"Alien ratatouille. I hope all the vegetables I used were actually vegetables and not... well, let's forget about that incident."

Qong laughed raucously. "We will never forget the time you used bryven innards to bake a cake." He waved at me. "Hello there. I'm Qong. You must be Pria."

I waved back before realising I was waving my knife at him. That could easily be misunderstood. "Hi. I've heard a lot about you."

Penny snorted while Fay whispered, "Waffles!", underneath her breath.

The ratatouille wasn't quite what I would have expected back home, but it was still delicious, especially after not having enough to eat on Kalumbu. While the others broke into light banter, I simply listened and ate. As soon as I emptied my plate, Silus snatched it away to refill it. He clearly had some sort of urge to provide for me, even if it hadn't been him who'd done the cooking.

When everyone was done - which took a while because the guys needed several portions each - Vruhag got up, his expression turning serious.

"Now that we're all together, we need to talk about our next steps. I'd planned to do this on the bridge, but maybe this is better. Now that we're all sated, we can think more clearly."

"Does anyone want a snack?" Fay asked when her mate paused. "I find making plans much easier with chocolate."

"Chocolate!" I exclaimed before I could stop myself. "You have actual chocolate?"

"Alien chocolate, even better than the real thing. Vruhag, would you be a darling?"

The orc gave the other males a long-suffering look, but obediently collected a glass box from a cupboard. He offered it to Fay first, who rewarded him with a peck on the cheek. Those two were truly adorable.

"Don't worry about it being blue, it still tastes like it should," Fay told me before nudging her mate to offer me the box. Inside it were small aquamarine cubes, not much bigger than dice. I took one and gave it a nibble. Velvety chocolate syrup filled my mouth. I realised the two women were watching me, waiting for my reaction.

"This is amazing!"

They grinned, clearly pleased.

Penny assembled her chocolate dice into a little wall in front of her. "We'll wait until tomorrow to tell you what it actually is. Take another. Or several. I know they say not to play with your food, but we're all adults here. Playing with food is allowed."

Vruhag cleared his throat. "Can we be serious now?"

21 SILUS

After days of not having anyone around me but Pria, it was strange to be surrounded by other people. Males in particular. Every time Vruhag or Qong looked at my mate, I tensed up. They tried their best to keep their distance, knowing exactly what it felt like to be a male who hadn't claimed his mate yet, but sitting at the same table with them was hard. I wanted to pull Pria onto my lap, both to feel her body against mine and to show a clear sign to everyone else, but I didn't want to overwhelm her.

She'd broken down completely and let me be a witness to her grief. I'd been honoured that she'd let me stay with her. It was proof of her trust in me. I'd feared that she might push me away, blame me even for her loss, but she'd coped much better than I'd anticipated. After falling in her strange battle trance where she'd stretched and bent her body, I'd been allowed to hold her. It had been a beautiful moment, despite the tragedy.

It would take time for her to cope with her grief. Both Penny and Fay still hadn't quite got over it, no matter how brave they seemed on the outside. You didn't just lose everyone you'd ever known and lived on like you had before. But I was glad the three females had each other. They all seemed of a similar age, so hopefully they'd become friends quickly. I wanted Pria to have the support of other females, even though it meant she'd have less time to spend with me.

The future was uncertain. We'd have to see what happened next. How we'd cope. When I'd get to claim her.

"Now that Silus is back and has successfully retrieved Pria, we have to consider our next steps," Vruhag began. "We know there is at least one more Peritan female to rescue. She may already be inside the Trials. We've set up a rudimentary monitoring system to scan all footage for her, but we also have to continue to take shifts to manually watch the Trials. Silus, Pria, I understand if you'd prefer not to for a while. We need you to hack into their systems again anyway, Silus, and search for any information on how many Peritans they took. We also need to find a new way onto the planet's surface. We can't assume that we'll have help again next time."

"Help?" I asked sharply. "What kind of help?"

"Our original plan had been to distract their security with the Bloodstar while I slipped through in the shuttle," the orc explained. "But they caught on fast. I was about to give up and return to the ship when someone sent me an encrypted message. A moment later, their barrier went off for just long enough for me to pass. The same happened on the way back."

"I want to see your communication log. We might have a friend on the inside. I was let onto the planet in the same way. I'd almost convinced myself that it had been the game makers, one of their traps, but if that mystery helper let you in and then out again... it could be a valuable ally."

Vruhag tapped his commband. "I've sent you all my logs. You've also got full admin access to the shuttle; in case you need to manually check its computers. Should we try to contact this potential ally?"

"It could still be a trap," Qong sighed. "They might be trying to get all of us, not just one or two. What's the likelihood of someone decent working on the space station?"

Penny waved her hands. "They could be like me and forced to work for the Trials owners. I never had a choice. It was work at the station or be ejected out of the air lock. Or worse. So I vote to give them a chance to prove themselves. If they're helping us, they're doing it for a reason. They must have some sort of goal. Maybe we can find out what that is."

"Can you contact them, Silus?" Vruhag asked.

"I can try. On the shuttle, I didn't have the time to look at the code in more detail. Maybe they left some sort of signature that can identify them. Or a calling card. Some hackers do that. Just give me a workstation and I'll do my best."

"Excellent. The rest of us will scour the Trials footage for another sign of the female. Pria-"

"I will join you," my mate said in a tone that left no doubt her mind was set. "I want to help."

Penny gave her a wide smile. "If you think you're ready, so be it. But first, we need to get you some clothes and a commband. And I bet you'd like a shower after Kalumbu. Or a swim?"

"Swimming sounds heavenly, as long as there are no tentacle crocodiles in the water."

"Tentacle what? Please tell me you didn't actually see one of those on Kalumbu."

The three females left after Qong agreed to start watching footage. Pria waved at me with a smile before following the other two Peritans out of the room. Hopefully this would keep her distracted from her grief.

Vruhag showed me to the bridge. He explained that there were in fact two command centres on the Bloodstar, one on each end, but the other was only for emergencies should this part of the ship be damaged.

"You can work over here. You should have all administrative rights, but let me know if something doesn't work. And please don't hack into the Bloodstar and start a mutiny."

He gave me a wry grin.

"Just because I worked for Twim doesn't mean I'm a pirate. He just offered the best pay."

"I totally understand. I've worked for people I would have preferred not to, but sometimes mercenaries can't be choosers. As I said, let me know if you need anything. I'll be doing some course adjustments before joining Qong."

The console he'd assigned to me was faster than Twim's best computer. Vruhag had really hit the jackpot when he'd acquired the Bloodstar. Everything was the latest tech and of the highest standard.

I pulled up the Bloodstar's shuttle communication logs first. The shuttle I'd crashed on Kalumbu may have sent some data to the cloud, but Twim had likely revoked my access privileges and hacking the firewalls I'd designed myself would take time. Of course there was a loophole I could use to get in, I always left one for situations like this, but I had to prioritise.

Scrolling through the lines of code was a familiar task that I enjoyed. It helped me get into that special zone where I was completely concentrated on a single task and could forget about everything around me. The communication log mostly contained automatic pings between the shuttle and the Bloodstar, as well as a conversation between Vruhag and Fay that I skipped. I didn't want to invade their privacy. Finally, I got to a very familiar line.

>>xs8f0ajfhofa You are welcome ja9000a=fgagjx[<<

I couldn't be entirely sure, but it looked almost exactly like the code I'd seen flash up on my own shuttle's screen. What did the letters and numbers around the message mean? Were they just random or was there a deeper meaning?

Time passed quickly as I tried all sorts of decryption methods. Occasionally, I thought of Pria. What was she doing now? Was she still swimming? Was she naked in the water? I wished I could be with her instead of working, but I knew that this was essential if we wanted to save another life. Another female destined to die on Kalumbu if we didn't stop the game makers.

I knew that even once we rescued her - once, not if - it wasn't going to be the end. We couldn't just leave knowing that others may be suffering the same fate. The game makers had abducted an entire group of females from an underdeveloped planet. Who was to say there weren't others in the same situation? No, we had to put a stop to them. Somehow, we had to take on the Trials of Kalumbu.

A shudder went down my back. I was a brave, battle-hardened satyr, yet the thought of just the six of us against one of the most powerful, richest crime conglomerates in the galaxy made even me shiver with worry.

22 PRIA

Watching Kalumbu on screen was a strange, an out-of-body experience of sorts. I'd only seen a tiny part of the planet, but whichever live stream I looked at, it all looked scarily familiar. The tall trees, even though their colours varied, the predators, the constant search for safety. The terrified faces of contestants as they battled yet another monster. I saw several of them die in just the first few minutes. Even though I'd been on the surface of that planet for days, I hadn't realised just how deadly it really was. How many lives it claimed every single day. Without Silus, I wouldn't have lasted an hour.

After a while, I skipped the deaths, unable to watch yet another person die. It was too close to home. That could have been me. Or Silus. Or Vruhag or Fay.

With every minute of watching the Trials, I got angrier at the game makers. They were doing this to make money. They were killing people, even if they didn't land the killing blows themselves. Kalumbu's earth was drenched in blood and what for? It had to stop. Not just to save any other humans who were still out there, but anyone who'd been thrown into the Trials against their will.

I took a break for dinner with Fay. Silus was still on the bridge, probably working hard, and I didn't want to distract him, even though I really wanted a hug from my satyr. Penny had taken the next shift of watching the Trials, armed with snacks and a large blanket. I'd not seen Vruhag and Qong since lunch, but I had a feeling they were keeping their distance. Silus' doing, no doubt. I'd seen the way he'd glared at them whenever one had dared to even look at me. He really had to work on that possessive streak. Or maybe not. I kind of liked it. Silus looked at me as if I was the only woman in the universe. I'd never had anyone look at me like that before. And maybe, yes, maybe, he could be the only man in the universe for me.

Was I moving too fast? I swallowed my embarrassment and asked Fay.

"How long did it take you and Vruhag to... you know..."

She laughed, a slight blush rising to her cheeks. "Not very long. Aliens seem to move a lot faster when it comes to dating. But it was a little different with Vruhag. Orcs go into a sort of mating fever and if they don't claim their mates, they can go mad, even die. So I didn't have a choice, I couldn't wait any longer. Not that I regret it, not in the slightest. He's the best thing that ever happened to me. Back home, I would have preferred a slower sort of dating, but here, it was right to jump into the unknown and just go for it."

"No regrets at all?" I asked.

"None. Actually, sometimes I wish I'd given in to our bond faster. It's my fault that he ended up crazed with mating fever. I shouldn't have waited as long. But then, we were on Kalumbu. You know what it's like. Not exactly a place to hold hands and have romantic dates."

I cringed, but forced a laugh. "Yes, not the most romantic of planets."

Was Silus going to be affected by this mating fever? He hadn't mentioned anything. Surely, he would, right? He wouldn't just suffer in silence... no, he would. That was exactly what he'd do if he thought it was in my best interest. Stupid man. I'd have to ask him, make sure.

In this moment, I realised I'd made up my mind. I wanted to be with him. Forever.

To test my resolve, I imagined other guys, men I'd fancied in the past. Their images passed through my mind and I felt nothing. Absolutely nothing. I couldn't imagine being with any of them. Not anymore. Silus was the one. And I had to tell him.

"Fay, can you send a message to Silus and ask him to meet me in our room as soon as he's done with work?"

She grinned knowingly. "Of course. I'll tell him to hurry up."

"No! Let him do his job first. It's more important than this."

"You're too rational. You should be drooling with-"

I thrust one of the green dumplings at her. "No! Stop. Eat this. Don't say things like that."

Fay flashed me an evil smile. "You know I'm right. Now go and get ready. Want me to get you some sexy lingerie from the fabricator?"

My immediate reaction was to say no, but then I reconsidered. "Only if you don't breathe a word about this to anyone."

She ran her fingers across her mouth. "Zipped. My lips are sealed. Let's get you ready for your sexy satyr."

I hadn't realised just how much I'd craved a shower after watching the Trials. Seeing those poor contestants die had made me feel dirty. But now that I was clean and wearing the skimpy lingerie Fay had made for me, I tried hard not to think of Kalumbu any longer.

Thin lacy panties revealed more than they hid, while the equally tiny bra barely covered my breasts. It certainly didn't offer the same support as the sports bras I was used to. Fay had chosen a dark blue colour for me that reminded me of the Atlantic Ocean in autumn. I had to admit that it looked beautiful against my skin. The few times I'd bought lingerie myself, I'd gone for white or black simply because that was what most people seemed to go for, but this deep blue complemented my skin tone much better.

The room was warm enough that I was able to sit on the bed without having to cover myself in a blanket. The glasses on the table had been magically refilled and more snacks had reappeared as well. The same flowers still stood in their vase, adding some colour to the room. Everything was ready.

Had Fay forgotten to send Silus my message or was he simply too busy to join me?

I rolled onto my back and looked up at the ceiling. A screen took up almost the entire space above the bed. We could watch movies here while snuggling. I could see us retreat to our cabin in the evenings, just the two of us, like a proper couple.

A gentle knock on the door made me sit up straight. Silus. I quickly checked that my bra was still hiding all the important bits.

"Come on in!"

The door slid open. Light blazed in from the corridor, turning the satyr into a hulking silhouette. His tail was held aloft, something I'd rarely seen him do before. Most of the time, I forgot he even had a tail because he usually had it wrapped around one of his legs so that it didn't get in the way. Or maybe he'd done that to make himself look less alien, less scary.

Silus sucked in a sharp breath when he saw what I was wearing. My cheeks turned hot as I felt his gaze wander over my body. He'd seen me naked for days. This wasn't anything new. But somehow, I felt more exposed than back on Kalumbu. Maybe because this time, it was my choice. I chose to present myself to him like this. I wanted him to see me vulnerable, open, seductive.

The door closed behind him. Now it was just us.

"I don't know what these garments are called, but I love them." His voice was deliciously hoarse. I wanted him to say all sorts of naughty things in that voice, whisper them as he pushed into me.

His hands went to the belt holding his loincloth in place, but I stopped him.

"Wait. Let me.'"

I moved to the edge of the bed and waited for him to approach. His erection tented the thick fabric of his loincloth. Finally, I'd get to see what he was hiding underneath.

I fumbled with the clasp of his belt, unfamiliar with the way it worked, but figured it out just when he tried to help. Our fingers touched, his warm and calloused, mine slender and slightly trembling. With the belt loose, I pushed it down over his hips, then let it drop to the floor. His cock awaited me in all its alien glory. The bulbous tip glistened in the dim light of the cabin. It almost looked like a large pearl held in place by a dark brown stem. His shaft was completely smooth, not a vein in sight, and - oh my goodness - what was that? I had to count. Six balls surrounded the cock, the same size as the pearl at the tip, covered in silky skin. All around his cock, thick fur covered his skin, but his cock and balls were completely smooth. Were those his actual balls or something else? I had so many questions, but I didn't want to ruin the mood by talking about anatomy.

The pearl at the top seemed too big to fit inside me. The longer I looked at it, the more it looked like an egg in its nest rather than a pearl. Nobody had mentioned egg-laying aliens.

"...Silus?"

"Yes, my mate?"

"You don't lay eggs, do you?"

He didn't laugh about my silly question. "No, I do not. Is that a problem?"

"What? No, not at all. I was a bit worried... I mean, it would be no problem if you did, I'd accept you no matter... anyway. Sorry. Ignore everything I just said."

This time, he chuckled softly. "I'm glad we got that sorted."

I forced the egg-laying theory out of my mind and focused on his cock again. With a quick look up at Silus, I wrapped my hand around his shaft. It felt even smoother than it looked, warm and hard. My fingers easily slid up and down his cock. When my pinkie touched the balls, they quivered in response. Unsure if I'd just imagined that, I touched them again, a little more forceful this time. They vibrated. Fuck me. These were going to be rubbing against my clit.

"The harder you push, the harder they sing," Silus muttered.

"Sing?"

"It's what the vibration is called. I assume our ancestors wanted to find a prosaic way of talking about it. The Great Song of Mates, it is called."

"That's kind of pretty."

"Not as pretty as you."

I looked up at him. His attention was fully on me, the intensity of his gaze scorching. I had to look away before I got distracted.

I moved my hand up his shaft again, pleased at the deep groans my touch pulled from Silus. The smooth skin formed a sort of bowl in which the pearl lay. I closed my hand around it, amazed at how the skin suddenly smoothed over the pearl. At the centre of it, a tiny drop of pre-cum gathered. I bent down and licked it. Not salty like I'd expected, more herbal. Thyme, just like his scent, with the tiniest hint of smoke. It was a masculine, earthy sort of taste that matched the man in front of me.

I swirled my tongue around the pearl, earning yet more barely suppressed groans. He liked it. So did I. My panties were soaked. My nipples strained against the lacy bra. And we hadn't even got started.

"I need you," Silus breathed. "Now."

In response, I tried to take him into my mouth. I'd only ever done that once before, with a guy I thought would be the perfect boyfriend, only he turned out to be married. I didn't really know what I was doing, but it felt right. The pearl shivered against my tongue, gentle vibrations that had its own irregular rhythm. A song. I listened to it with my tongue, soaking in the vibrations while gently rubbing my hand up and down his shaft. The longer I stayed like that, the more I could image hearing an actual melody. A song as old as time itself, telling of the love of two people brought together by fate. I didn't want it to end. The song made me want to feel this love, this miraculous connection. It told me the way to end that craving. And I was ready.

With one last swirl of my tongue around the pearl, I sat up and looked straight at Silus. My mate.

"Claim me."

23 SILUS

She was the most wonderful creature in the universe and she didn't even know it. When she wrapped her fingers around my cock, I wanted to throw her onto her back and claim her. But I resisted the urge. Slow. I didn't want it to be over too fast. This moment would never come again. Our first claiming. The moment we'd become one in the name of the stars and the ancestors. I had to find my self-control and not behave like a horny youngling.

She now lowered herself on her back, her legs invitingly spread. My cock was harder than ever, ready to sing the song of songs inside of her. But something wasn't quite right. I'd deal with that dainty fabric clinging to her wet mound in a moment, but first I had to free her breasts. They were covered in a dark blue fabric that reminded me of stormy autumn nights back home on Faunus. Tiny holes revealed her skin underneath, but they weren't enough. I needed to see everything. I wanted my mate bare in front of me, just like I was now fully exposed to her. Tonight, we'd bare our souls and our bodies to each other and become one.

I didn't even attempt to look for a clasp or fastening. I slipped one finger underneath the flimsy garment, right between her breasts, and slowly let my nail grow into a claw. I ripped through the fabric, letting her breasts spill free. They were just the right size, each fitting into my hand, inviting me to squeeze and caress. I couldn't resist leaning down and planting a wet kiss on both nipples. They puckered beneath my touch, hard yet pliable. If I hadn't been so impatient, I would have taken the time to suck them properly, but I would save it for later. The night was still young. I had told Vruhag not to expect me in the morning. I'd done more work than I'd planned today so that I would be able to spend as much time with my mate as possible.

Keeping my lips hovering above her smooth skin, I moved down, kiss by kiss, until I reached the indentation that had fascinated me from the start. I swirled my tongue around it, exploring that strange hole.

To my surprise, Pria giggled. "That tickles!"

Amused at her reaction, I teased that spot a little more before moving downwards. Her scent was sweet and heady, driving me crazy with need. I would taste her later. Now, I had to claim her before I spilled myself on the sheets.

I shredded her undergarment with my claw before sheathing it again, making sure I wouldn't accidentally hurt my mate in the heat of the moment. I discarded the pieces of fabric, hoping that it had come from the fabricator and could be replicated. I wanted her to wear them again, every day, and rip them off her repeatedly. There was something primal about revealing her beautiful body bit by bit.

She looked at me with big eyes, her lips slightly parted. I could have kissed these lips for an eternity and still feel like I hadn't got enough. Her taste was like a memory of every good moment of my life, come together into this burst of sweetness. But no, again, that was for later.

I stared into her eyes and asked the all-important question. "Will you be my mate?"

Her lips quivered slightly when she responded. "Yes."

It wasn't the official response of my people, but that didn't matter. She wanted me. I wanted her. That was enough for me.

I spread her thighs a little more until her glistening centre lay ripe before me. My cock throbbed with need. I positioned myself against her entrance, my songbud eagerly vibrating at the contact. One more time, I met her eyes, and keeping eye contact, I slowly pushed into her. She was tight, but not painfully so. I took my time, giving her a pause to adjust, then pushing in a little further. She swallowed me greedily, taking me into her sanctum until my cocklace touched her entrance. She was made for me, or I for her. I was fully embedded, unable to push in any further, and that was exactly where my cocklace started. Yet more proof that we were meant to be together.

A ripple went through me when the cocklace began its song. It had never sung this loudly before. The melody was transmitted through my bones, resonating up my spine all the way to my ears. Without thinking, I pulled out and pushed in again to the rhythm only the two of us could hear. I never quite understood why they called it the Song of Mates, but now I knew. This song would only ever sound when two mates claimed each other, I was sure of it.

The song increased its pace and so did I, slamming into her core while our eyes remained locked. Pria's mouth was open and she moaned in rhythm to the song. I realised I was doing the same, in between heavy breaths. I was tumbling towards the end, my cock twitching and aching with the urge to release myself into my mate. I should try to hold on for a bit longer, lengthen the pleasure for Pria, but she looked like she was close to the edge as well. Her gasps were short and sharp, her fingers clawing at the sheets, her back arched.

Linked by our bodies and our song, we hurtled over the cliff in unison, her screaming her release as she contracted around me, while I roared as my seed shot deep into her. My cocklace continued humming against her, prolonging her orgasm, making her twitch around me, while I stayed deeply embedded within my mate, enjoying the feeling of completeness.

The room around me suddenly felt more colourful. Life itself was more vibrant. It seemed that my life until now hadn't been the real thing, only now did I see that.

Pria hummed softly, the melody of the song, an echo of our joining. I smiled, my eyes stinging with emotion. My hearts beat only for her. She was my everything. I slowly slid out of her and lay alongside my mate, kissing her flushed lips.

"Atm," I whispered. "You're my atm now. My one true mate, my breath, my soul, my life."

We kissed, our tongues dancing to the echo of our song, a melody nobody else would ever hear, our secret from now until the day we turned into stardust.

Pria was amazed to learn that each pearl on my cocklace meant one orgasm. Apparently, Peritan males had less sexual prowess and were only able to come once or twice in a row. How pitiful. I delivered Pria five rounds of pleasure, until she fell asleep in my arms. When we woke up, I carried her into the cleansing room and helped her wake up properly by licking her until she came into my mouth.

"Do they refill quickly?" she asked after when we got dressed, pointing at my cocklace.

"By tonight, I will be ready to serve you in any way you desire," I promised. My cock was still hard, one pearl unspent. I considered taking her against the wall, but it was already after lunch and my sense of duty kicked in. As much as I wanted to lock us into this room and not leave for at least a week, we were in extraordinary circumstances. A life may depend on us. I promised both myself and my mate that once this was over, we'd go somewhere far, far away and do nothing but fuck, eat and sleep. Maybe a bit of talking, knowing Pria.

We arrived in the canteen just when Penny started a ship-wide announcement. She stopped as soon as she saw us enter, waving excitedly.

"Perfect timing. We have food and news. Sit down, you two must be starving."

She wiggled her eyebrows in a strange way. For some reason, that made Pria squeeze my hand. I clearly needed to learn a lot more about Peritans if I ever wanted to understand all their weird little habits.

Pria moved to sit on one of the chairs, but I pulled her onto my lap.

She gave me a stern look. "Only today. Tomorrow, I'm sitting on my own."

I sighed. "If you must. But know that my lap is always open for you."

"I shall remember that." She laughed. "What's the news?"

Fay handed out the food while Vruhag gave us a report of what we'd missed.

"We spotted the Peritan female on a new episode of the Trials. Just for a moment in the background, but all of us have watched the clip and are sure that it's a Peritan. And you were right, Silus. The programme you wrote worked."

"What programme?" Pria asked, and I realised I'd never filled her in on what I'd done all day before our claiming.

"After I looked at the communications log, I found a pattern in the transmission that we received from one of the local comms satellites. It's mostly used for ships to synchronise their clocks and help with long-range communication across space, but someone very, very clever embedded a signal. Whenever a ship gets close to the barriers around Kalumbu, that signal triggers a subroutine which alerts whoever is listening for it. That means the person who helped us through the blockade isn't necessarily on the Kalumbu space station. They don't need the game makers' surveillance equipment to know that a ship is close, they just have to check their programme. Although the fact that they managed to open the barrier for us does suggest that they're on the station. Anyway, I wrote a programme that simulates a ship approaching Kalumbu. I embedded a message in the hope that our mysterious hacker would see it."

"And they did," Vruhag boomed, raising his glass. He'd learned that gesture from his mate. We all had. It seemed a fitting way to celebrate, raising glasses like battle axes. "We got a reply."

Everyone's attention was on the orc. He must not have told anyone until now.

"What did it say?" Penny asked.

Vruhag grinned. "It's an invitation."

EPILOGUE

VENOM

I have done all I can do.

I have watched her. I have protected her. And when they broke through my deceptions and found her, I called for help. Now all I can do is wait.

I am not like the orc and the satyr. I cannot take part in the Trials. I cannot fly to Kalumbu and be a hero. I am stuck in my role, pretending to be worse than the worst of them, while my heart darkens and my soul withers. I have to stay here among those who would harm her.

I will stay in the shadows. I will watch. And only once the time is right, I will strike.

I am Venom.

I am her mate.

This is the end of Silus and Pria's story, but they will reappear in My Big Scaly Alien Naga, *along with the rest of the Bloodstar crew and of course Venom and his human mate.*

If you're new to this series, find out how Penny and Qong met in My Big Sweet Waffle Monster:
skyemackinnon.com/wafflemonster

THE STARLIGHT UNIVERSE

This book is part of the Starlight Universe, an entire galaxy filled with hunky aliens, exotic planets, and the human women ready to find love among the stars.

Starlight Highlanders Mail Order Brides

Alien Highlanders in kilts come to Earth in search of brides... and take them to planet Albya. Three m/f standalones full of humour, action and steamy romance. Part of the Intergalactic Dating Agency.

The Intergalactic Guide to Humans

A humorous take on alien abductions, probing and other shenanigans. One reverse harem trilogy about clueless aliens and the human woman they abducted, followed by several standalone romances with various pairings (m/f, f/m/f and m/m). If you want light entertainment filled with unicorns, fabulous misunderstandings and unusual body parts, this is the series for you.

Starlight Vikings

Set on Earth and on the spaceship Valkyr, this trilogy of m/f standalones is all about hunky alien Vikings in need of females. Part of the Intergalactic Dating Agency.

Starlight Monsters

These aliens are not your usual humanoids… they have claws, fangs, tails, scales, knotty dicks and will growl at you. Interconnected m/f standalones with lots of action, steam and fated mates.

ABOUT THE AUTHOR

Skye MacKinnon is a Scottish romance author who was raised by elves in the mystical Highlands and calls the Loch Ness monster her friend. Her bestselling books weave together romance with action, suspense and whimsical humour, creating page-turners filled with strong heroines, alpha heroes and loveable monsters.

Whether she's writing about aliens in kilts, hunky Vikings or cat shifter assassins, Skye likes to put a new spin on familiar tropes. Some of her heroines don't have to choose, some fall in love with other women, and others get abducted by clueless aliens.

Skye lives with her bossy cat on the west coast of Scotland and uses the dramatic views from her office as an inspiration, no matter whether she writes fantasy, paranormal or science fiction romance. Until she gets abducted by aliens, that is.

Subscribe to her newsletter:

skyemackinnon.com/newsletter

ALSO BY

Find all of Skye's books on her website, **skyemackinnon.com**, where you can also order signed paperbacks and swag.

Many of her books are available as audiobooks.

SCIENCE FICTION ROMANCE

Set in the Starlight Universe

- **Starlight Vikings** (sci-fi m/f romance)
- **Starlight Monsters** (sci-fi m/f romance)
- **Starlight Highlanders Mail Order Brides** (sci-fi m/f romance, part of the Intergalactic Dating Agency)
- **The Intergalactic Guide to Humans** (sci-fi romance with various pairings)
- **Starlight Mermen** (sci-fi m/f romance)

Set in other worlds

- **Between Rebels** (sci-fi reverse harem set in the

Planet Athion shared world)

- **The Mars Diaries** (sci-fi reverse harem)
- **Aliens and Animals** (f/f sci-fi romance co-written with Arizona Tape)

PARANORMAL & FANTASY ROMANCE

- **Claiming Her Bears** (post-apocalyptic shifter reverse harem)
- **Daughter of Winter** (fantasy reverse harem)
- **Catnip Assassins** (urban fantasy reverse harem)
- **Infernal Descent** (paranormal reverse harem based on Dante's Inferno, co-written with Bea Paige)
- **Seven Wardens** (fantasy reverse harem co-written with Laura Greenwood)
- **The Lost Siren** (post-apocalyptic, paranormal reverse harem co-written with Liza Street)

OTHER SERIES

- **Academy of Time** (time travel academy standalones, reverse harem and m/f)
- **Defiance** (contemporary reverse harem with a hint of thriller/suspense)

STANDALONES

- Song of Souls – m/f fantasy romance, fairy tale retelling

- Their Hybrid – steampunk reverse harem
- Partridge in the P.E.A.R. - sci-fi reverse harem
  co-written with Arizona Tape
- Highland Butterflies – sapphic romance
- Wings of Time and Fate - epic fantasy

ANTHOLOGIES AND BOX SETS

- Hungry for More – charity cookbook
- Daggers & Destiny – a fantasy romance starter
  library
- Stars & Seduction - a science fiction romance
  starter library